Caroline Fothergill

Put to the Proof

Vol. I

Caroline Fothergill

Put to the Proof
Vol. I

ISBN/EAN: 9783337066246

Printed in Europe, USA, Canada, Australia, Japan

Cover: Foto ©Andreas Hilbeck / pixelio.de

More available books at **www.hansebooks.com**

PUT TO THE PROOF.

A NOVEL.

BY

CAROLINE FOTHERGILL.

" Fair, kind and true."
SHAKESPEARE.

IN THREE VOLUMES.
VOL. I.

LONDON:
RICHARD BENTLEY AND SON,
Publishers in Ordinary to Her Majesty the Queen.

1883.

PUT TO THE PROOF.

CHAPTER I.

" This beggar-maid shall be my queen."

SQUIRE TERRY had quarrelled with his son :
it was impossible to doubt it. Dent, the
footman, had been crossing the hall when
Mr. Eustace had left the house, and the
old servant had seen, from the expression
of his young master's face, that he had for
once made up his mind, and would be
every whit as determined as his father.
A few minutes later Dent had been summoned to Mr. Terry in the library, and had

any doubt on the subject been lingering in his mind, it must have been dispelled by what he saw and heard. Mr. Terry was seated in his own particular chair, his elbows resting on the arms, his hands tightly clasped, a look of invincible determination on his handsome, obstinate face. He had given a few orders respecting Mr. Eustace. His things were to be packed that they might be despatched at a moment's notice to any address the young gentleman might send; his name was never to be mentioned in his father's presence.

Dent left his master with a heart heavy and sorrowful. It had come to this, then. The young master, whom he had led by the hand and made much of when he was a child, had been driven from his home because he would not marry the woman whom his father had chosen for his wife.

"Dear, dear," murmured the old man, shaking his head as he made his way from the library to his own quarters, "it is a pity; yet he never could abear Miss Agatha, and for two years he has been nigh crazed about this Margaret Shuttleworth. It will be an ill day when the Squire of Ash Fell comes to marry a mill hand, and yet I doubt she'll make a fonder wife than Miss Agatha."

The relations of these four people to one another may be quickly traced. Mr., or Squire Terry, as in the neighbourhood of his estate he was more generally called, was lord of the manor of Ash Fell. For centuries the family had ruled over the broad lands appertaining to it, and had dwelt in the stately mansion which formed the chief feature of the place. The house had been altered, repaired, and restored till little remained of the original fabric, and the present dwelling-place of the Terrys was a handsome structure of no particular period or style of architecture. It stood on a raised terrace, and was immediately surrounded by gardens, tastefully and quaintly laid out; while beyond the gardens, away on all sides spread the park, remarkable on account both of its size and beauty.

Robert Terry, the present lord of the manor, had only one child, his son Eustace. He had been married twice; Eustace was the son of his first wife. The second Mrs. Terry had borne him no children; she was a widow with one daughter, who had married and gone out to India with her husband. So much for the dwellers of the Hall.

The girl of whom Dent had spoken as

" Miss Agatha " was Mr. Terry's ward, Agatha Flintoft, a young lady some four years younger than Eustace, and who had grown up with him from a child. An heiress and an only child, Mr. Terry had looked upon her as in every way a fitting match for his son. He had not given much consideration to the question whether the young people loved one another or not. If he thought at all of their respective characters, it was to reflect that Agatha's energy and decision of character would weigh well in the balance against his son's dreamy, unpractical ways.

Last, but by no means least, factor in this problem was Margaret Shuttleworth. Neither heiress nor gently born, the only resemblance her circumstances bore to those of Miss Flintoft lay in the fact that she, too, was an only child. Her father

(her mother had been dead many years) was a weaver; one of the many men who some ten years before had come from the surrounding villages to work in the cotton factory, which was then a complete innovation in that part of the country, and is still the only one for miles around. Margaret was a child when her father first settled at Ash Fell, and she had always been his companion in his rambles on the moors and hills, in which he employed the greater part of the time which was not spent in the mill. In this way she had met Eustace, who was also addicted to ramblings amongst the hills. The boy and girl might almost be said to have grown up together, and as they grew older the brotherly and sisterly feeling which had always existed between them gradually changed its character, with the result which has been seen. Eustace, who during the twenty-four years of his life had obeyed his father implicitly, when at last commanded to take the most important step in his life and get him a wife, refused the well-born damsel his father had chosen for him, and announced in decided terms his intention of marrying the other companion of his youth, Margaret, daughter of Ben Shuttleworth, the weaver. The result has already been described.

Eustace knew, when the door of his father's house closed behind him, that he had left his home for ever. He knew that, if he persisted in marrying the woman he loved, his father would never relent, but would carry out his sentence of banishment for life to the letter; but he did not flinch. In proportion to his habitual want of stability and weakness of purpose was his present fixed determination to have his own way in this matter. He had counted the cost, and was prepared to accept the consequences of his defiance to their full extent. When he left his father's house, therefore, he went straight to the cottage where Margaret lived. He told her all that had passed between his father and himself, overruled her scruples as to how far she was justified in being the occasion of a quarrel between father and son, and finally won her consent to the publishing of the banns for the first time on the following Sunday.

A month later the Squire received a communication from his son, containing a formal notice of his marriage with Margaret Shuttleworth.

Mr. Terry read the notice composedly. He was alone breakfasting when he received it. After breakfast he sent for his lawyer, and a week later Eustace had no more legal claim upon his father than the most complete stranger.

CHAPTER II.

"Men do not think of sons and daughters when they fall in love."

TEN years had passed since Mr. Terry disowned his son, and Eustace lay upon his death-bed. Two years before his wife had died, and Eustace, too weak and broken to survive the loss long, had wandered from one place to another, taking with him his little girl, named Margaret after her mother, and finally returning to the place where he had buried his wife, had settled himself there to die.

He was lying in bed, looking very feeble; the most casual observer would have seen that his last moments had come. The doctor who had attended Mrs. Terry through her last illness was seated by the bedside, receiving the dying man's last instructions. Eustace held a letter in his hand, about which he was apparently speaking.

" You will post this, please, as soon as possible after I am gone. You will be doing me a great kindness. It is to my father. Ten years ago, when I married, we quarrelled, and we have held no communication since.". He paused a moment for breath, and went on, " My little Margaret will very soon have no other living relative, and I have written to tell him I am dying, and to ask him to receive her. I do not think he can refuse, though I feel keenly the humiliation of having to make the request; but it is the only thing that can be done for her. All my things will, of course, belong to her; I have no money to leave her. The woman of this house has kindly consented to let the child remain here until she hears from her grandfather. I think that is all."

"Pardon me, Mr. Terry," said the doctor quickly; "did I understand you to say that my little friend Margaret is to remain here alone?"

"Yes; I am afraid she will be very miserable, but it is the only place there is."

"You must let me take her home with me: she will be better among my little ones. Nay, I will take no refusal; it is a settled thing."

"You are very good," said Eustace, feebly; "I cannot thank you sufficiently for all your kindness." He was interrupted by a violent fit of coughing, which exhausted him; when he had rested a few moments, he went on—

"Now, will you call Margaret? I must see her."

In answer to the doctor's summons a little girl entered the room. She was tall for her eight years, and her golden hair shone in the sunlight.

"Does papa want me?" she inquired.

"Yes," said Dr. Turner; and going from the room, he left father and daughter together.

Eustace talked to the child for a long time. She knew her father was dying, and her face wore an expression of sad gravity mingled with awe. At the end of an hour she was told to call Dr. Turner, and a few minutes later Margaret was an orphan, alone in the world.

Dr. Turner took her home with him, and

she stayed with his family until a letter came from her grandfather, stating his willingness to take her into his house, and requesting that she might be sent to Ash Fell on the following day.

Margaret, then, was sent to Ash Fell to her father's old home, to live with the grandfather with whom she already felt a certain degree of familiarity, having often heard his name from Eustace, and in the latter days many details concerning his character and the place where he lived.

I have said that Mr. Terry expressed his willingness to take charge of Margaret; the word was misapplied. He did it most unwillingly. He had got his son's letter, and for a day or two afterwards had felt no hesitation as to how he should act. He had certainly no intention of adopting his granddaughter. the child of " that woman " whom Eustace had married in spite of his commands. How did he know that the child's parents were really dead, and that it was not all a plot against him? Second thoughts, however, convinced him that his son must be dead; and after fighting against the conviction, he began to realize that the child possessed neither parents nor any living relative besides himself (Ben had died two or three years before). It seemed that he would have to maintain her, in any case. How should he dispose of her? His pride shrank from the idea of sending her to school, and letting the heiress of the house of Terry distinguish herself by manners and customs pertaining to a mill hand: the child, he thought, was sure to resemble her mother. He came at last to the conclusion that there was nothing for it but to have her at the Hall, and he reluctantly wrote to Dr. Turner to that effect.

It was a beautiful June evening when Margaret was set down on the platform of the little station at Ash Fell. Dr. Turner had told her that some one would meet her at her journey's end, and she looked inquiringly round as she stood by her box, when the train had moved out of the station. She saw no one, however, and so allowed her attentions to become absorbed in the contemplation of a pony-carriage standing just outside the station. She was wondering whether her grandfather would keep such pretty ponies, when she heard a voice far above her saying—

"Dear me! is this the child who is to come to Mr. Terry's?"

Margaret looked up, and, child though she was, she shrank from the tall woman who stood looking down upon her through her gold-rimmed eye-glasses.

It was Agatha Flintoft who had spoken, or rather Agatha Entwistle, for a year or two after Eustace had left home, she had bestowed herself and her fifteen thousand a year upon the Church, as represented by the bachelor vicar of Ash Fell. She was now the vicar's wife, and, as such, ruled her husband and the parish with a high hand. It was strange that she should be the first to address Eustace's child; perhaps it was not so strange that Margaret should shrink from the tall woman with sharp features and harsh voice, who stood before her. Nevertheless, she answered with grave directness—

" Yes, I am Margaret Terry. Has any one come to meet me, please ? "

Mrs. Entwistle glanced around the station, saying—

"It would seem not."

Then turning to the railway company in general, she inquired whether any one had come from the Hall to meet Miss Terry.

She was assured with promptitude that no one had been, so she turned to Margaret with a shrug of the shoulders.

"It seems no one has come, child. I am driving past the Hall, and will take you with me; but your box must be sent for. I cannot have it in the phaeton."

And in spite of this generous offer, Margaret still shrank from her.

They reached the Hall in about a quarter of an hour. Mrs. Entwistle did not alight, but handed Margaret over to the care of the housekeeper, with a brief explanation of how she had met the child.

Margaret was led through passages which appeared to her numerous and of great

length, to the housekeeper's room, where
she was bidden to rest and partake of the
tea provided for her. When she had
finished, the housekeeper took her into the
little bedroom which had been provided
for her, and subjected her to a tidying
process. The short, waving, golden hair
was brushed afresh, the pale little face
bore the application of soap and water, and
then she was pronounced to be ready.

Margaret had been very silent all this
time; now, however, she looked up into
Mrs. Fenton's face, and said—

"Where is Mr. Terry? Papa said I
was coming to live with him."

"You are going to see him now, my
honey," said the kind woman; and taking
the child by the hand, she led her away
to the library. "I have brought Miss
Margaret, sir, as you sent word," said Mrs.

Fenton when she and her *protegée* stood within the room.

Mrs. Fenton was not a person of tact, or she would have chosen some other way of introducing the child to her grandfather. The name " Margaret " only served to recall the woman who was the cause of the child's being there at all.

Mr. Terry evidently felt it so, for his eyebrows met in an ominous frown as he lowered his newspaper to greet his visitor. The frown deepened as he looked the child over from head to foot, and asked—

. " When did she come ? "

" It seems there was some mistake about the train, sir, and no one went to the station; but Mrs. Entwistle happened to be at the station, and she brought missy up."

She had seen that her master disliked

her previous mode of naming the child, and, old and privileged servant though she was, she did not venture to repeat the offence.

Mr. Terry nodded.

"You may go, Mrs. Fenton," he said. "Leave the child here; I will ring when I have done with her."

Mrs. Fenton went away, and the squire and his grandchild were left alone.

For a few moments the old man sat in silence. After a pause, he beckoned to the child, saying—

"Come nearer to me—quite close."

Margaret came and stood on the hearth-rug, at the side of her companion.

"Not there, child; in front, where I can see you," he said harshly; and, taking her by the arm, he placed her immediately in front of him.

Then, still keeping his hold on her arm, he leaned forward and narrowly scanned every feature of the face before him. Margaret bore the scrutiny in silence, looking with her candid, childish eyes straight into the old man's face. Unconsciously he tightened his hold on her arm, until she made an involuntary movement to free herself, saying—

"Please, let me go. You hurt me when you hold me so tight."

The sound of her voice seemed to break the spell. Mr. Terry let go her arm, and with a short laugh threw himself back in his chair, while his eyebrows lowered more darkly than before.

What he saw before him only increased the anger he already felt against his granddaughter. Had Margaret resembled her father, the squire might have tolerated though he could never have loved her.

But in face and form she was her mother's
daughter. The childish voice even sounded
like an echo of Margaret Shuttleworth's
clear, full tones. Nor did the likeness cease
there. Her very name was that of the
beautiful weaver who had lured Eustace
from the paths of filial duty and obedience.
There was but little chance that a personal
interview with her would soften Mr.
Terry's heart towards his granddaughter.

The old man threw himself back in his
chair and remained silent, gazing out of
the window. He was considering what he
should do with Margaret, now that he was
unavoidably burdened with her. He would
never endure her in his presence, and he
had decided not to send her to school;
neither could she live in the housekeeper's
room. It seemed that she must be educated
at home. He could not, however, endure

the thought of having a governess in his house—governesses invariably made mischief wherever they went. He would engage a tutor, some young man, small matter whom, provided he could read and write, and would keep the child out of his way. He would advertise in the *Times*, that would give him least trouble.

So far he had got in his meditations, when he was startled by the sound of a clear small voice, which said—

"I am so tired of standing; may I go now, please?"

He turned round with a start. Though he had been thinking of the child, he had utterly forgotten her presence. Now he felt a kind of shock at the sight of her.

"I thought you were gone," he said. "Ring the bell."

Margaret obeyed, and directly afterwards Mrs. Fenton appeared.

"You may take the child away," said her master. "I have a few directions to give about her. I wish that her name may never be mentioned to me. I want to have no more to do with her than I am obliged. Keep her out of my sight, and tell the servants she is to be called 'Miss Terry.'"

"Yes, sir," answered Mrs. Fenton.

"I shall engage a tutor for her," he went on. "She will live with him up-stairs. Those rooms Mr. Eustace had in the east gallery may be put in order. Let the child remain there till her tutor comes."

"Yes, sir," again said Mrs. Fenton.

"That is all," he concluded; and Mrs. Fenton withdrew, taking Margaret with her, and feeling it very hard that the sins of the father should be so visited upon the child.

The following day the rooms in the east gallery, consisting of a sitting and two bedrooms, were swept and garnished, and Margaret was installed in them in solitary dignity.

That same day Mr. Terry advertised in the *Times* for a tutor for his granddaughter.

CHAPTER III.

"A fine young man,
  . . . Although the sun of youth
Has shone too straight upon his brain, I know,
And fevered him with dreams of doing good."

IN one of the suburbs of London, in a handsomely furnished room, sat a lady, engaged in plain sewing. Near her sat two little girls, aged respectively six and seven years. One, apparently the eldest, was hemming a pocket-handkerchief, and, to judge from the puckered, sorrowful little face and the long piece of work which bore signs of frequent unpicking, the pocket-handkerchief was a source of trouble to her.

The younger girl was ostensibly doing a tiny addition sum, but the slate, which was held well hidden from the eyes of her mother, was covered with drawings of birds, beasts, and men. The elder child kept steadily at her work, though now and then she heaved a little sigh of sorrow; the younger was continually looking out of the window into the sunny garden, though she never committed such a breach of discipline without first stealing an interrogative look at her mother.

Mrs. Welford was, however, too much occupied with her own thoughts to give her customary meed of attention to her little girls, and so Elsa's frivolity and Madge's sulkiness escaped remark for once.

Mrs. Welford's thoughts were very dismal and unhappy, and, if she had uttered them aloud, would probably have run something like this:

"What new craze has that boy got into his head now? It seems no use arguing him out of one folly, for he is sure to run straight into another. For the last three months he has been raving about the education of girls, abusing what he calls the 'criminal methods' now in vogue, and imploring me to hand over Madge and Elsa to him." Here she looked up, and seeing that Elsa's attention had wandered to the garden, sternly requested her to draw down the blind. "But I think I know better than that. It is all his father's work. He indulged Philip frightfully, and let him read what books he chose: this is the result."

She paused for a moment to examine Madge's sewing, and then went on thinking.

"Instead of turning his mind to some

useful profession—for though he is under no necessity to work for his living, a man should always have some settled occupation —he has taken it into his head that he has a vocation for bringing about what he calls "the higher education of women," and Margaret encourages him in it. He has begun to talk about getting a post as tutor, or setting up classes for girls. Heaven knows where it will all end! He will break my heart. The education that was high enough for me is high enough for my daughters, I imagine. He has been so strange and reserved all this week, he can only be meditating some fresh plan. Surely that was his ring. Madge, go and open the door for your brother."

Madge obeyed, and soon returned, followed by a young man, who came toward Mrs. Welford, saying—

"Good morning, mother! It was so fine this morning, I could not wait for the family breakfast, but set off for a walk into the country. I was miles away by eight o'clock."

Mrs. Welford glanced at the clock, which at that moment struck twelve.

"Have you been walking until now?" she asked, with a tinge of sarcasm in her voice.

"No; I have been with Aunt Margaret for some time. I had some news for her, and I want to talk it over with you now."

"Always your aunt before your mother, Philip. You are greatly wanting in respect."

"It is not that, mother," said the young man, his face clouding. "I was coming home, and met the postman close to Aunt Margaret's, and I naturally went in to her first."

" I want no excuses," she said, displeased
and jealous. Her only son, who would
have loved her if she would have let him,
had always chosen her sister as his *confidante* in preference to herself. Mrs.
Welford had not the confidence of her
children, and she knew it.

" And what is this letter you were going
to tell me about ? " she asked at length.

Philip looked at his little sisters.

" Let the children go," he said, " and
then we can talk quietly."

Madge and Elsa received permission to
put away their work, and in five minutes
Philip and his mother were alone. Philip
was just drawing the letter of which he
had spoken from his pocket, when his
mother rose in her calm, deliberate way,
saying—

" You must wait a moment, Philip ; I

have something to tell cook. I shall not be long."

Philip, ever attentive, crossed the room and opened the door for her; then returned to the fireplace, and, leaning against the mantelpiece, began to whistle.

He was a fine, tall young fellow who had attained his majority some months previously. His figure was slight; though he had broad shoulders, he did not look as if he would ever be a stout man. His face was thin and dark and eager, and the extreme mobility of his features suggested what he in fact possessed, a quick and fiery temper. His forehead was that of a thinker; his grey eyes, so dark as to be almost black, were singularly quick and penetrating. The mouth and chin were good.

Philip, as he leaned against the chimney-piece and looked out of the window, of which he had drawn up the blind on first entering the room, unfolded the letter he had taken from his pocket, and began to read it, and as he read his face hardened. He knew that his mother would be violently opposed to the step he meant to take, and he felt he should require all his own most convincing logic, and his aunt's most soothing words, to overcome her objections. But he had no fear as to the result. Latterly, he had had many trials of strength with his mother, and the victory had always remained with himself.

At this point Mrs. Welford re-entered the room. She did not speak until she was seated in her own particular chair, and had taken up her sewing, then she said—

"Now, Philip, I am at liberty to hear what you have to say."

" Yes. ' There was a pause of some minutes' duration, then he went on. " You know that I have been talking for some time about education. I believe I have found out where the fault of the present system lies. I think I can point out why it is that our women are so frivolous, so little to be trusted in serious matters."

" Considering to whom you are speaking, I regard your words as strangely wanting in respect," said Mrs. Welford, frigidly.

Philip's eyebrows contracted. He never talked long with his mother without losing ais temper.

" You know I am not alluding to you in any way, mother. I mean the generality of girls one sees nowadays. Take the average schoolgirl, for instance, and tell me how far the training she receives at an average boarding-school—— "

Mrs. Welford waved her hand.

"Spare me all that, Philip," she said. "You have expressed your views on that topic very often at great length; my memory stands in no need of refreshment."

"I have spoken, too, of getting a post as tutor, or work of a similar kind." (Mrs. Welford smiled derisively, and yet her heart began to beat more quickly; she had a vague idea that her son's words might be tending to deeds at last.) "A few days ago I saw an advertisement in the *Times;* a tutor was wanted for a little girl of eight. I answered the advertisement; my application was successful; the post is mine."

Philip paused. Mrs. Welford sat silent; but, as Philip said no more, she felt constrained to speak. She therefore asked—

"Am I to understand that you have accepted a situation as tutor?"

"Yes."

She did not speak for some little time. She had never really believed that Philip would carry out the project which she knew had long been half formed in his mind. In thinking over the matter to herself, she had always been filled with righteous indignation against her son; but when it came to the point, when she found another preferred before herself as her son's *confidante*, her indignation was changed to disappointment, and for the moment she could not speak. When she did her voice was not quite steady, and she spoke in a lower tone than usual.

"I do not know whether to be surprised at what you tell me, Philip. You have talked about this kind of thing very often

of late, but I was hardly prepared to find
you so indifferent about acting in opposition to my wishes. I have no legal right
to prevent you from taking this step, but I
thought that would have inspired you with
greater respect for the moral obligation
you owe me. The position of the man of
a family determines that of his sisters or
other relations, and the future of your
sisters has to be thought of as well as that
of this unknown child, to whom you are so
willing to dedicate your time. I had
always looked forward to your filling a
very different position in life from that of
a tutor, and if you persist in this plan it
will be a great disappointment to me."

While she had been speaking, Philip
had abandoned his position in front of the
hearth, and begun to pace up and down
the room. His mother's words were not

without effect ; that is, though he was re-
solved not to give up his plan, he began to
see that it was not a matter concerning only
himself. A feeling came over him that to
a certain extent his mother had a right to
feel disappointed ; and just at the moment
when he was going to offend all her
prejudices, he realized how dear she was
to him, and how it hurt him to set aside
her wishes.

"Mother," he said suddenly, pausing
near her and impulsively laying one hand
on her arm, "I am sorry if you are disappointed. I do not want to vex you ; but
you would not have me lead an idle life.
You condemn all young men who waste
their time in that way."

"No one hates idleness more than I do ;
but teaching is not the only profession
open to a young man. Why will you not

study for the Church or medicine ? In
either of those professions you might earn
distinction, which you never will do as a
tutor."

Unfortunately, Mrs. Welford had not
been able to keep entirely out of her voice
the contempt she felt for the profession her
son wished to adopt, and the slight con-
veyed in her tone roused Philip's anger.
His colour was deeper than usual as he
replied—

"Public distinction one may never earn,
but the distinction that lies in training a
child to a high ideal in life, may be won
by any teacher."

"I do not see," said his mother, a half
smile parting her lips, "how you are to
inspire any one with a high ideal when
you disobey your mother's wishes."

"Ah, mother ! you see after all it lies

with you to make or mar my career. How could I succeed without your approval, and you will not let me fail when I might succeed?"

Philip, as he spoke, bent and knelt on one knee by his mother, and looked up into her face with his fine dark eyes. He was, and always would be, her favourite child. From his childhood she had always given way to him, and though this last freak of his was more distasteful to her than any other one had been, she felt that she could not withstand him. She laid her hand upon his hair, and her hard mouth relaxed into a smile, as she replied—

"The old story, Philip; you take unfair advantage of me. It is a pity you will not go into the Church. You would get whatever you chose from your congregation."

Long experience had taught Philip to know the precise point in a discussion at which his mother yielded to him, and now his only answer was—

"Thank you, mother. If it is not in every way a most desirable post, I promise you I will not stay."

The fight was fought, and Philip was victor. It had always been so. His mother made a valiant resistance at first, but always yielded in the end. Philip told her where he was going, and they spent half an hour talking over it, and parted the best of friends.

Philip journeyed to Ash Fell the day but one following his discussion with his mother. He was full of hope, and though he understood the importance of what he was doing, he was not afraid of failure; whence, perhaps, arose his success.

It was not a month since Mrs. Entwistle
had driven Margaret up to the Hall, when a
dogcart stood at the station, waiting for the
train by which Philip was travelling. It
was not many minutes late, and the
numerous clocks about the place were
striking six as the dogcart drew up in
front of the Hall.

Philip asked for Mr. Terry, and was
shown into the library, where the squire
sat writing. For a moment the old man
seemed at a loss to account for the presence
of his visitor, but he recollected himself,
and apologized for his forgetfulness. He
asked Philip to join him at dinner.

" I want you to understand the position
you will occupy here." He paused a
moment, and then, reflecting that sooner
or later Philip must hear of Margaret's
parentage, he went on to give in a few

words the reason for his presence in his
house. "You and I shall not meet often,"
he concluded, "but when we do, I do not
wish your pupil's name to be mentioned to
me. I desire to hear nothing about her.
She must be educated, and with that view
I have engaged a tutor for her."

Dinner was finished almost in silence.
Mr. Terry, being accustomed to live alone,
seemed to have forgotten his companion's
presence. At last they rose from table.

"Why did you select me for this post?"
asked Philip, as they parted.

"Your application reached me the first."
He had rung as he spoke, and to the
servant who answered the bell he said,
"Show Mr. Welford to his rooms."

Philip followed the man till he came to
a door, at which he knocked.

"Come in," said a childish voice; and

the man, pushing open the door, announced—

"Mr. Welford, miss."

Philip, as he entered, saw a child's figure rise from the window-seat, and a little girl came forward ánd held out her hand shyly, saying—

"How do you do, Mr. Welford?"

Philip, with Mr. Terry's harsh words still in his ears, felt a rush of pity at the sight of the child sitting alone in her black frock in this large gloomy room, for it looked gloomy just then. He bent down and kissed the child's forehead, asking—

"Are you my little pupil?"

"Yes," said Margaret. "Mrs. Fenton told me you were coming."

"Who is Mrs. Fenton?"

"The housekeeper."

Philip had now seated himself in the window, and, drawing the child to him, he began to talk to her. They talked until it was time for Margaret to go to bed, and Philip was left alone.

He sat still in the window-seat, looking out into the soft summer gloaming and thinking of his new circumstances. Mr. Terry's behaviour seemed to him in the last degree heartless. Margaret he thought the most charming child he had ever seen, and her old-fashioned name, having no disagreeable associations for him, struck him as very pretty. He was glad that he should have his little pupil all to himself, though he could not like the reason which had been given for the arrangement. From the window where he sat, he could see through the trees the chimney of the obnoxious cotton-mill; and Margaret, in child-like innocence had told him, " That chimney belongs to the mill where mamma worked before she married papa. She was called Margaret, too."

CHAPTER IV.

> " Golden-haired,
> Grey-eyed, and simple.
>
> *   *   *   *
>
> A very maid, yet fearing not for aught."

IT was a still afternoon in July. The sun shone hotly down on the country round Ash Fell, ripening the corn and turning the apples from green to red or russet brown. Ash Fell Hall slept in the sunshine; nearly all the blinds were drawn; no one was moving in the gardens or about the stables.

Along the road which wound past the Hall in one direction on to the moor, in the other through the village of Ash Fell to the neighbouring town some four or five miles distant, a man and a girl were riding. They rode very slowly: it was too hot to make rapidity of movement desirable, even had it been necessary. No one but Philip Welford could own that dark, thin face, with eager, restless eyes and mobile mouth. He is ten years older than when we saw him last; the enthusiastic youth has merged into the earnest, thoughtful man, but the expression of his face is not much altered.

The girl at his side, then, must be Margaret, whom we last saw as a child of eight, shyly welcoming her tutor. It is more difficult to recognize her, for the pretty child has developed into a stately maiden of eighteen, who certainly has but little of the appearance of an ordinary schoolgirl. If the object of Philip's system

of education was to produce a young lady
who should bear little outward signs of the
general type of girlhood, he has admirably
succeeded. Margaret looks a year or two
older than she really is, but this is probably
as much owing to her tall, splendidly developed figure, and the dignified, graceful
carriage of her head, as to the thoughtful
expression of her face. Her hair is like
her mother's, yellow as gold ; her eyes,

> " Too expressive to be blue,
> Too lovely to be grey,"

look steadfastly out from under her level
dark eyebrows ; her complexion, slightly
flushed with exercise, is no whit less
delicate than when she was a child; her
mouth is no rosebud, but the lips are red
as coral, and though their general expression is rather grave than gay, she is laughing at present.

"I wish we did not always meet Mrs. Entwistle when we go out," Philip was saying; "the mere sight of her puts me into an evil frame of mind for the rest of the day."

And Margaret laughed as she answered. "You should not look at her, Mr. Welford. It is foolish to expose one's self to temptation without necessity."

"My dear child," he said, "you are speaking at random. Have you considered what the cost of such a step would be? Mrs. Entwistle would think I wished to insult her, and her husband would call and demand satisfaction. You don't like her any better than I do."

"I never have liked her. We might take turns at avoiding her. I thought she looked at us more superciliously than usual to-day."

They rode on in silence. They were returning from town, where Margaret had been shopping. As Mr. Terry never allowed her to have any money in her own possession, she was always accompanied by Philip, who paid for the things she bought, and afterwards sent in his bills to the squire. It was a simple way of doing business, and one which gave Mr. Terry no trouble, it being perfectly understood that Margaret's expenditure was strictly limited; but it was very unsatisfactory to the girl herself.

Mr. Terry would have had his granddaughter brought up in complete ignorance of money matters, had he been able, but here Philip circumvented him. In one of his rare interviews with Mr. Terry, he had been told that in all probability Margaret would inherit her grandfather's property at his death. Eustace had been an only child, and though Mr. Terry could leave the property as he would, Margaret was his only living relative except his step-daughter, Mrs. Latimer, with whom he had never been able to agree. It was, therefore, highly improbable that the old man would make a will in her favour.

When Philip knew this, he had, in direct disobedience to Mr. Terry's wishes, taken upon himself to instruct Margaret as to the duties and responsibilities of her future position, as mistress of a large estate, with fifteen thousand a year at her own disposal. It did not harmonize with his scheme of education that the girl should be brought up without ever having held so much as ten shillings in her own possession, and suddenly find herself one of the richest women in the county. His instructions had not been in vain. Margaret, having grown up in the knowledge that one day most of the country lying for some miles around Ash Fell would be her own, often pictured herself in her grandfather's position, and laid plans for what she would do in the future.

She was thinking of this now, as she rode along and saw the dirty children as they played in the village street or greeted herself and her companion with shrill cheers as they passed by. She was wondering whether the children would be so fond of playing in the dirt, and the men of lounging about, when she had instituted a public gymnasium; and whether the women, who stood gossiping at the cottage doors, would be so hopelessly dirty and untidy when the village was provided with baths free of charge.

As she thus mused, she heard a horse
coming along in the direction opposite to
that in which she and her tutor were
going. She looked up. The rider was an
old man, on a chestnut horse, closely
followed by a large retriever. As he passed
he raised his hat in silence ; she, in return,
bowed without smiling ; Philip raised his
hat, and then he was gone, and the road
before them was empty once more.

"There was Mr. Terry going for an
afternoon ride," she remarked. "I wonder,"
she went on, after a pause, "what Mr.
Terry does all day ? His life must be very
lonely."

"He is used to it," said Philip; "and
there is the farm to look after, and the
estate, and no end of things to see to ; and
when all these joys pall, there is always
Mrs. Entwistle."

"True," said Margaret, half smiling, "there is always Mrs. Entwistle."

And with that they rode in at the gates, Philip helped her from her horse, and they went indoors.

Meanwhile, Mr. Terry rode on, thinking. It was not once in three months that he happened to meet Margaret; whenever he did see her, the sight disturbed him. She was so very like her mother. To-day he could almost have believed it was Margaret Shuttleworth he had seen riding along the village street. The squire had only lately returned from London, where he had been spending some weeks, and he seemed to see Margaret with new eyes. He recognized that she was no longer a child, but a young woman, and—he had to swallow the pill, bitter though it was—a very beautiful woman. He did not know how old she was;

he had kept no count of her years, but he thought she must be sixteen or seventeen.

He rode on until he reached the Vicarage. He had not meant to call, but Mrs. Entwistle, who saw him, called to him, and he had to obey. Perhaps the only soft place in the old man's heart was that occupied by Agatha Entwistle. He had known her since she was a child, and had loved her as though she had been his daughter—much more than his step-daughter, now Mrs. Latimer, with whom he had never been able to get on, and every one knew it. When Mrs. Entwistle called to him, therefore, he turned his horse in at the gate, and reined up in front of the window out of which the lady was leaning.

"Good afternoon, Agatha," he said, raising his hat.

"Good afternoon. I am having five

o'clock tea, and am quite alone; the vicar cannot come. Won't you relieve my solitude?"

"I can't refuse," said the old man gallantly; "a lady's society is a treat I do not often enjoy."

"You should have Margaret down in the evening to make tea for you. It is quite time she left the schoolroom, and saw a little society."

The squire looked so little pleased at this suggestion that Mrs. Entwistle went on quickly—

"Now, don't look cross. I called you in because I want to talk to you about the girl; so come into the house and have your tea in comfort."

She began to pour it out as she spoke; and the squire, seeing nothing for it but to obey, threw his horse's bridle over the top of a little wicket-gate leading into another part of the garden, and entered the house.

"I met Margaret this afternoon," began his hostess, almost as soon as he had seated himself.

"So did I."

"She was riding with her tutor. What is his name? Welford," she went on, superciliously.

"Ay," remarked the squire. The subject did not seem to possess any particular interest for him.

"How old is Margaret?" pursued the lady.

"I don't know; sixteen or seventeen, I dare say."

"She is eighteen," said Mrs. Entwistle, concisely; "and at eighteen a girl is old enough to leave the schoolroom. Margaret can have done little else than learn lessons for the last ten years, and even if she is not very bright, she ought by this time to know quite as much as her mother's daughter needs to know."

"How do you know she is not very bright?" asked the squire, who always seized upon unexpected points in a discussion.

Mrs. Entwistle shrugged her shoulders and raised her eyebrows.

"I know nothing about her mental powers, of course," she drawled; "but she is so like her mother physically, that I cannot but think she resembles her mentally, and we all know how deficient the lower orders are in brain power."

Mr. Terry smiled sarcastically.

"At any rate, her mother possessed sufficient brain power to successfully plan out a scheme for getting her child into my house," he growled.

"I have only just got back from Scotland, as you know, and it is some months since I saw Margaret. I thought her greatly changed to-day; she has a much more 'grown-up' appearance than I remember having noticed before. She will be a very handsome woman."

"She is her mother over again," said the squire, sharply.

"So far as I remember, her mother was a very handsome woman," said Mrs. Entwistle, coolly. "Margaret's is a kind of beauty that attracts many men, though I confess she is too big for my taste; still, when she is introduced, she will no doubt make a great sensation."

The squire was silent, though he looked displeased. He did not love Margaret, and

her beauty was no source of pride and
delight to him. If she had only had the
delicate, fragile loveliness of the Terrys,
instead of the strong, noble beauty of a
daughter of the people, her fate might have
been different.

Mrs. Entwistle looked rather impatiently
at Mr. Terry as he sat in silence. So far
she had not been successful, the squire had
taken her words according to their outward
meaning, and did not seem to consider that
they might have any hidden significance.
Presently she spoke again.

" About how old is Mr. Welford ? "

Mr. Terry stared a little.

" Upon my word, my dear," he said, " I
have no idea; I should think from his appearance, he may be one or two and thirty.
I remember when he first came he told me
his age, but I do not know how long ago
that is."

"Two and thirty," murmured Agatha, meditatively, "and Margaret is eighteen; a susceptible age when one has seen nothing of the world."

Mr. Terry looked up quickly.

"My dear Agatha," he said, and his tone would have been contemptuous if he had been speaking to any one else, "are you going to suggest an attachment between my granddaughter and her tutor? Remember he is in my service; the fellow can't be so presumptuous as that!"

Agatha raised her eyebrows again.

"You see, considering who her mother was, it would not be so wonderful, after all."

"Still, she is Miss Terry."

"And will some day be very rich. Excuse my mentioning it, but we must always look at things in all their lights.

Some day Margaret will have fifteen thousand a year. Mr. Welford must be very short-sighted if he has lost sight of that."

Mr. Terry set down his teacup and clasped his hands.

"This must be seen to," he said, "and at once. I confess, such a possibility never suggested itself to me; it requires a woman's eye to ferret out these things."

Whether he spoke sarcastically or not Agatha did not inquire; she only said—

"I am afraid I have made you uneasy, but these things happen so often. One can never be sufficiently on one's guard."

"You did quite right. I shall speak to Welford to-night."

"Do nothing rash," she said. "I don't want you to act on the impulse of the moment, and then to feel that you might have done better in leaving things alone."

"No, no; I shall not be acting in a hurry. He has been here quite long enough; he shall go in three months. I shall speak to him to-night."

Mrs. Entwistle, having set things going according to her wishes, abandoned the subject of Margaret's future, and she and her old friend sat talking about matters of local interest until he rose to go, and rode away, after thanking Agatha for having put him on his guard against Philip Welford.

Philip and Margaret spent their evening in their usual manner. Philip never allowed his pupil to study at night; she devoted her evenings to books of a lighter character, or to needlework.

This evening Philip had been reading aloud. They were finishing "Felix Holt," and during the reading of the last few pages Margaret had dropped her work in her

lap and sat listening breathlessly. When
Mr. Welford closed the book, she looked
up with the light of enthusiasm shining
in her face.

"That is good," she said. "I do not
know when I have enjoyed a book so
much. How one grows to love Esther.
She would have been miserable if she had
married Harold."

"How do you make that out?" said
Philip.

"Their natures were so dissimilar, and
she would have found it out before
long."

"But at the beginning of the book their
characters have always struck me as being
strangely alike. If she had not married
Felix, her character would not have developed. As Harold's wife she would have
made no progress, she would never have

known what was in herself, and would have been quite happy."

Margaret shook her head. " The change had come when she met Harold, or she would not have given up her claim to him, and she did not know then that Felix would ever ask her to marry him."

"True," said Philip, and the discussion dropped. Margaret took up her work again, and Philip turned over the leaves of the book, reading to himself a passage here and there.

Margaret fell into a dream. She felt very happy and contented ; she had grown to love her life. Philip was her friend more than her tutor. Looking back over the years they had spent together, she found only pleasure, and again pleasure in the retrospect. The presence and influence of Philip were in every act of her life, almost

as far back as she could remember. How
pleasant he had made those years! Her
heart glowed with the warmth of friendship as she thought of him. She could
not think of her life without him; it would
be very dreary. Looking up suddenly, she
said—

"It will be ten years to-morrow since
you came here, Mr. Welford."

"Indeed," said Philip, smiling, though
he did not raise his eyes from his book.
"Has the time seemed long or short?"

She laughed. "How can I answer such
a question? It has been ten years of
my life. I don't know whether life goes
quickly or slowly. I want to be certain
about one thing," she went on, after a
pause.

"What is that?"

"Don't you remember telling me, when

you had taught me all you know about wood-carving—— "

" Ah!" said Philip, interrupting. " You are not quite certain whether I spoke the truth when I said I had taught you till you could carve better than myself. I suppose it makes one quite dizzy to realize that one knows more of any subject than one's teacher."

He spoke in a tone of kindly mockery; and Margaret laughed as she answered—

"It is you who remind me of it, not I you. I was not going to say that at all. I know you are too sensitive on that point. What you said was that every girl ought to be taught some occupation by which she might support herself, if need were. I am not sure that I could support myself by wood-carving. You admire my things, but you are my teacher. I should like to

know what an impartial judge thinks of
them, and whether they would be bought
if I offered them for sale. How can I find
out?"

Philip laid down his book.

"I don't know," he said, "what I have
done that you should lose all faith in my
judgment. Bring the things here, and let
us look at them."

She left the room, and presently returned,
carrying in her strong, white hands a large
box, which she set upon the table, and
together they emptied it of its contents.
The table was presently strewn with
carvings. There were many things—photograph frames, book-slides, and numbers of
other articles, both large and small. Philip
examined them carefully. They were
exquisitely carved. Some of the designs
were his, some her own, but in every case

they were carefully and minutely executed; a competent judge would have said there was not only talent, but genius displayed in the work.

"You are very sceptical," said Philip, smiling. "However, to convince you, I will send some of your things to the dealer in London who used to dispose of my carvings. I shall not say anything to bias his judgment; I shall tell him to keep the things, and send me what he thinks they are worth. I can depend upon his honesty."

When Philip sat alone reading, after Margaret had gone to bed, a servant came to him with a message from Mr. Terry, who requested his presence in the library.

Philip involuntarily glanced at the time-piece. It was eleven o'clock; rather an unseasonable hour, he thought, for an inter-view. He told the man, however, that he would come, and, having finished the chapter he was reading, closed the book and went downstairs.

Mr. Terry was writing when Philip entered the library, but he laid down his pen and courteously enough requested the young man to be seated. Then he plunged straight into the business of the hour.

" I believe," he began, " that my grand-daughter is now eighteen years of age."

Philip assented, and he went on—

" It is time she left the schoolroom. Girls are usually supposed to have finished their education " (Philip's eyebrows con-tracted ; the expression was particularly disagreeable to him) " at a somewhat earlier age, but "—he hardly liked to own that he had thought Margaret to be a year or two younger than she really was ;

fortunately, Mrs. Entwistle's suggestion occurred to him, and he went boldly on— " but in my granddaughter's case, I was willing to prolong her school life that she might have a better chance of making up for any natural want of intelligence."

Philip's surprise could not be restrained.

" Do I understand you to speak of want of intelligence ? Margaret is highly gifted in every way."

" Do you always call her Margaret ? " asked the old man, with a sudden flash of suspicion.

" Of course," hardly knowing whether to laugh or be angry.

" My granddaughter is usually called Miss Terry."

Philip sat in puzzled silence. He did not in the least understand the squire's manner. In all his former interviews,

which did not number more than two or
three, Philip had always called his pupil
by her christian name, and it had never
excited any remark. It would have passed
unnoticed now but for Mrs. Entwistle's
warning.

"However, to return to my point" ("It
is a relief," thought Philip, "to find he has
a point"), "I was talking to Mrs. Entwistle to-day." (Philip looked up quickly,
and almost said, "Ah!") "She agrees
with me that it is time Miss Terry should
be introduced into society. I believe that
when you first came here we agreed that,
in the event of either of us wishing to end
the engagement, a notice of three months
was to be given on either side."

"Yes," said Philip, rather absently. He
was thinking of Margaret.

"Then, you will consider it as settled,

that after three months I shall no longer require your services."

Mr. Terry then went on to make various polite speeches as to the friendly relations that had always existed between himself and Mr. Welford, the confidence he had reposed in him, etc. To all these things the tutor made only vague and unsatisfactory replies, and somewhat abruptly wishing his employer, " Good night," left the room.

Philip went upstairs to his sitting-room, and there threw himself into a chair and sat thinking.

It had come to this at last. Of course he had known that sometime Margaret would be grown-up, and he would have to go. Nevertheless, when the time did come, he was foolish enough to feel that it was rather hard. It was Mrs. Entwistle who

had suggested this, and it was just like
her. Had nothing to the contrary been
suggested to him, the squire would have
allowed Margaret's present mode of life to
continue until his death, with no thought
that any change might be advisable.
" Mrs. Entwistle had agreed with him ! "
It was much more likely that he had agreed
with Mrs. Entwistle. Poor little Margaret!
She would hardly have a pleasant life,
spent as it would be in the society of a
man who detested her, with the alternative
of that of Mrs. Entwistle. He hated to
think of it, but it was characteristic of
Philip that he did not think of a marriage
for Margaret as a solution of the difficulty.
He supposed he must tell her. The sooner
she knew the better, but she should have
the next day free from care. It is so much
easier to bear one's grief at night, when

one may creep away, bury one's aching head in the pillow, and hide in a dark corner from the eyes of the curious, than in the morning, when there is a long glaring day of work and thought before one. To-morrow, too, was a festival ; she should enjoy that, the last, in peace. And with these thoughts running in his mind, he went to bed.

CHAPTER V.

" Blow, west wind, by the lonely mound,
    And murmur, summer streams;
  There is no need of other sound
    To soothe my lady's dreams."

PHILIP had said on the preceding night
that the next day was a festival, which
Margaret should celebrate before hearing
that they were to be separated.

It was a very harmless festival, and consisted of the celebration of the anniversary
of Philip's coming to Ash Fell. They had
observed nine of these anniversaries, this
was to be the tenth and last. The custom
had grown up very naturally. When
Philip had been at Ash Fell a year, Margaret

had asked for a holiday, and had proposed that they should spend it among the hills. The same thing had happened on the two following years, by which time it had become a rooted article of their faith, and was never departed from.

Philip was in the sitting-room first that morning. It was a lovely morning, and he stood by the window, thinking how Margaret would enjoy herself.

At that moment he heard a light step behind him, and, turning, saw Margaret. He bade her " Good morning," and laughingly reprimanded her for being late. To which she made answer—

" Do not imagine you were here first. I have been ready for some time, but I went into the garden to get these flowers. Are they not lovely ? " and she held her basket, piled to the top with roses, for him to see.

" Very beautiful," he said. " Are you
going to put them in water before breakfast ? "

" Yes," glancing at the table. " Morris
has not brought the coffee yet; " and collect-
ing her pots and glasses round her, she
began to fill them with roses.

Philip, as he leaned against the window
and looked at her, thought she was more
beautiful than any of the flowers she had
gathered. She looked very bright and
happy that morning. She had on a soft
white dress, and had fastened one dark red
rose, with its glossy green leaves, at her
throat. She pursued her work deftly and
swiftly, and had almost finished when
Morris, the schoolroom maid, brought in
breakfast.

" Wait one moment, Morris," said the
girl, " and you can take away these stalks

and leaves with you." Another moment and she set the glass in the middle of the table, saying to Philip, "Fresh flowers, you observe, in honour of the occasion."

They left the house soon after breakfast. They were going to spend the day at a place some miles away, famed for its beautiful scenery, and they carried specimen boxes, for they were going to botanize.

Quarter of an hour in the train brought them to Crag Towers. Here they left the train, and after walking for some time along the rough, uneven street of the little town, they turned off into a road which led through some woods to " The Enchanted Valley."

The Enchanted Valley was approached by a narrow road, one side of which rose up in tall cliffs, clothed with trees, while the other sloped down steeply and then

rose again, thus forming a narrow deep
ravine, at the bottom of which flowed a
swift mountain torrent. The valley itself
was shut in by hills on all sides—hills of no
great height, and which were in winter no
doubt bleak enough, but in the summer
and early autumn they glowed with the rich
hues of gorse and heather. Two streams
flowed through the valley, and joined their
waters under an old stone bridge, grey
with age, and overgrown with moss and
creeping plants and ferns.

This valley was a favourite place with
Margaret. She loved to come and sit by the
stream, listening to the unceasing swirl and
murmur of its tumbling waters. Whatever
trouble she might bring to the Enchanted
Valley, she never failed to find peace
within its limits.

When Philip and Margaret reached this

spot, Philip threw himself unto the soft, thick grass, and Margaret sat down on a little heathy mound by the side of the water, and gave herself up to meditation. Some words from " Wuthering Heights " were running in her head : " In winter nothing more dreary, in summer nothing more divine," and she felt there was no place in the world so beautiful as her native York-shire. She was so lost in thought that she forgot Philip, until the rustling of the leaves of a book roused her, and looking up, she said—

" What book have you got there, Mr. Welford ? "

" Emily Brontë's poems. Shall I read you one ? "

" Do. Her poems were chiefly written in places like this, and ought to be read out-of-doors."

Philip turned over the leaves. He did not seem to find what he was in search of. Presently he said—

" Here are three verses from one of the poems, which, as you say, might have been written here. How do you like them ?

> " ' The linnet in the rocky dells,
> The moor-lark in the air,
> The bee among the heather bells
> That hide my lady fair ;

> " ' The wild deer browse above her breast,
> The wild birds raise their brood ;
> And they, her smiles of love caressed,
> Have left her solitude.

> *　　　*　　　*　　　*

> " ' Blow, west wind, by the lonely mound,
> And murmur, summer streams ;
> There is no need of other sound
> To soothe my lady's dreams.' "

When he had finished there was silence. Margaret sat looking away over the "summer streams" on to the hills ; her face was almost solemn with her intensity of feeling.

" Oh," she said at last, " that is more beautiful than words can express! What one must feel to be able to write that! Do you feel as I do, that when you read such a poem in a place like this you long to cry ? "

" Certainly it stirs the very innermost depths of one's nature."

Margaret rose, and stood looking into the water. She had thrown away the rose that had nestled at her throat, and now wore a bunch of early heather; her hat lay on the ground beside her, and the sunlight played upon her golden hair. She was repeating the last verse Philip had read. The words seemed to have taken a strange hold of her ; she felt she should never forget them.

At last they turned to go. They climbed

the hills which shut in the Enchanted
Valley, and crossed the wide stretch of
open moorland which separated them from
the road by which they had come. It
was not a long walk to Crag Towers, but
it was a most beautiful one. They reached
home about eight o'clock, Philip feeling
he had a hard task before him; Margaret
with the dreamy happiness still lingering
about her. As she and her companion
reached their sitting-room, she said—

"I have never enjoyed any of our
festivals like this one. I shall never forget
to-day!"

Later on in the evening, she sat over her
wood-carving. She was engaged on a
work of some size—a hanging bookshelf
for presentation to her tutor on his birthday. She loved her work; it was an ever-
new delight to her to watch the design

take shape and grow beneath her fingers. Philip was writing to his Aunt Margaret, telling her that in three months he should have finished his work, and would be back in London.

When he had finished his letter, he looked at Margaret. He was half tempted not to tell her that night, she looked so happy; but he steeled himself to his task, and, leaning back in his chair, spoke aloud.

" I want to speak to you, Margaret."

She looked up.

" Yes; well, I can listen when I am carving."

" But what I am going to tell you is rather startling; you might make a mistake. I had rather you left off working."

She put down her tools, and, turning her chair, sat facing him.

" Last night," he began, " after you

were gone to bed, I had an interview with Mr. Terry."

"What had you to tell him?" she inquired, rather curiously.

"Nothing. He sent for me."

"Really?" almost incredulously. "What did he want?"

"He told me he had been talking to Mrs. Entwistle."

"Ah!" cried Margaret, uttering the same exclamation that had so nearly passed Philip's lips the night before.

"And they have agreed that, as you have attained the ripe age of eighteen years, it is time you left the schoolroom and began to go into society. They think you have finished your education," sarcastically.

She began to see his meaning, and her face went a shade paler.

"And—and what shall you do?" she asked hesitatingly, as though unwilling to have her own fear realized.

"Mr. Terry told me that, after three months, I shall no longer be required here."

"Are you going in three months?"

"I suppose so."

She covered her face with her hands in silence, while she gently rocked herself to and fro. It was a habit she had when in any kind of tribulation.

At first Philip did not speak; but this lasted so long, that at last he went up to her, and taking her hands from her face, he said, half laughing, half expostulating—

"My dear child, what is the matter?"

She raised her eyes to his; the tears were standing in them.

"Is it true?" she said. "What shall I do when you are gone?"

"You did not surely imagine we were going to live in this way all our lives?"

He spoke jestingly. He would not show his own sorrow, since it would only add to hers. But there was no answering smile upon her face, as she replied—

"No; I don't know what I thought, but I thought you would not go yet. You might have stayed until I was twenty-one."

She did not cry, but her face was very sad.

"You see, Mrs. Entwistle has decreed otherwise."

"Ah, Mrs. Entwistle!" she said, energetically; "it is just like her to do this. What does it matter to her if I have a tutor till I am an old woman, if Mr. Terry does not object? I am not her daughter."

"If you had been her daughter, you would never have had a tutor at all," said

Philip, laughing. "We must make the best of it; we have three months in which to say 'good-bye.'"

"And after the months are gone," she said, "how shall I live with Mr. Terry, who hates me, and with Mrs. Entwistle? I always said she was our enemy."

She paused suddenly, and hid her face in her hands, crying bitterly.

"Margaret!" cried Philip, "you must not do that. I cannot bear to see you cry. I hate the thought of going, but you will make it much worse for both of us if you cry like that."

"I cannot help it. What shall I do when you are gone, when there is no one to talk to, no one to tell me anything? Only Mr. Terry, who always looks as if he would like me to fall dead at his feet."

"My dear girl!" remonstrated Philip.

"He does indeed. He would be glad if I died. And I have to live with him instead of you. It is like—nay, there is nothing to compare it to ; it is too horrible ! "

Philip laughed at her again, and talked to her until she had ceased crying, and had even smiled faintly at some of the things he said. But she remained very sad, and soon went to her room, where she cried herself to sleep, for the first time since the death of her father.

Philip sat still, thinking. It was a hard wrench for him to part from Margaret. "She will soon get over it," he thought.

He then turned to his desk to finish the article he was writing for one of the current reviews, but his thoughts continually strayed off to Margaret, and to speculations as to her future; while his eyes, instead of keeping to the paper before him, were for ever roaming round the room where he had lived for ten years, taking in its most trivial detail of furniture or arrangement, and noting everything. Finally he found it impossible to fix his thoughts on the consideration of the Eastern Question, so he left his desk, and as the clock was striking midnight, he decided to go to bed.

As he passed Margaret's table, where she sat when at her wood-carving, he stooped to pick up something lying on the floor. It was the spray of heather she had worn that day, and he picked it up with a smile, and put it in his pocket-book, saying—

"I will keep this as a reminder of my little sister Margaret, and of our last festival."

From which remark we may conclude that Mrs. Entwistle's hints that Philip was seeking Margaret's fortune were quite unfounded.

CHAPTER VI.

"Oh, hard that we
Were once so full of all felicity!"

A WEEK had passed since Philip had broken to Margaret the tidings of his approaching departure, and she had had ample time to reconcile herself to the idea. That, however, she could not do. It seemed as though she had not been able to realize it at first, and every day, by shortening the time that remained to them, intensified her sorrow.

It was evening again, and again Margaret was at her table, busy with her carving. Philip was out; he had said he was going to the post-office, and so she was alone. She was working diligently, but presently she laid down her tools, and, leaning back in her chair, looked round the room with a loving, lingering gaze. What a dear old room it was! For ten years it had been her home, for she had never left Ash Fell since she first came there, except on one or two occasions, and Philip was intimately connected with both. Twice he had taken her away during her holidays. One summer they had spent a month at the Lakes—that was six years ago ; and again, two summers ago, they had travelled to the south of England, and made a walking tour through Cornwall and Devon. With the exception of these two months, this room had been her home since she had been eight years old.

It was a very pretty room, large and

rather low. The two low, broad-seated windows looked to the south-east, so that the room was ever bright with sun. The furniture had been collected from other parts of the house: scarcely two chairs were alike. On either side of the fireplace stood bookshelves of the kind called "dwarf," filled with books belonging to herself and Philip. On the top of each stood various pots and ornaments, also owned by both tenants of the room. Margaret, as she turned her serious eyes upon the shelves, thought how dreary they would look when only her books were in them, and when Philip's share of the pots was gone too. There was also, on one side of the room, a quaint old oak cabinet, black with age, and brilliant with the polish which Margaret never failed to make part of her day's work to bestow upon it.

The table at which she was sitting stood
in one of the windows, so that she might
have the full benefit of the light for her
work.

Her gaze, after travelling round the
room, returned to the window, and she
looked out over the trees till her eyes
caught the tall chimney of the mill, where
she had once told Philip " mamma worked
before she married papa."

Margaret was well acquainted with her
mother's history. She knew her exact
social position, and the light in which Mr.
Terry had regarded his son's marriage.
She had a miniature of her mother, and
knew how closely she resembled her. She
knew, too, that to that fact was to be
attributed a great deal of the aversion her
grandfather felt for her. She knew it all
very well; and during the last two or

three years, since she had been able to
think for herself, the subject of her father's
marriage had occupied a large place in her
thoughts. She had looked at it in all the
lights which had suggested themselves to
her, and she had talked it over with
Philip; but she had never been able to see
that her father had done wrong.

She knew that she owed her banishment
from her grandfather's presence to the
fact that he was ashamed of her, and the
thought made her heart swell with anger.

She was thinking of this now, as she
sat alone, watching the tall trees sway to
and fro in the evening breeze, and her
thoughts were bitter enough. They ran
somewhat like this :

" He has never given me a chance of
showing what I am, or whether I have my
father's character or my mother's; though,

indeed, he did not know what her character was. Mrs. Entwistle says he has been so good to me that I can never repay his kindness. I do not see it. I was an orphan, without a penny, and he was my only relative. How could he do otherwise than take me into his house? And, having done that, how could he do less for me than he has done? He has fed and lodged me, so he does the least of his servants; and to not one of them does he pay his wages with so grudging a spirit as he gives me a small allowance for my dress. Even that I might not keep myself: he has treated me as though I were an idiot or a thief."

She paused a moment in her growing excitement; then she went on.

" Perhaps I ought to be grateful for the good education I have had, but not to him. Mr. Welford has given me all that, and I am more grateful to him than I can express. He has been here ten years, and during those years he has spoken to Mr. Terry four times, twice my name was not mentioned. He cannot, and he does not, know what or how I have been taught; for anything he knows I have been taught no more than to read and write, perhaps not even that. If Mr. Welford had been an ignorant, rude, rough man, it would have been the same; he would have been here, and I might have lived my life as I could. It was a mere chance that Mr. Welford was what he is; it made no difference to Mr. Terry whether I was happy or not; he did not know and he did not care. Anything was good enough for the weaver's daughter. All he cared for was that he should never be annoyed by the sight of me."

Perhaps the only thing Margaret had
inherited from her father was a tendency
to deep fits of depression, when everything
grew black around her, and there seemed
no outlet from the gloomy labyrinth of her
thoughts.   Such fits came upon her without any warning, often without any greater
apparent reason than a hopelessly wet
day, or the sight (always an unwelcome
one) of Mr. Terry.   Sometimes they only
lasted for a few hours, sometimes she could
not free herself from them for days.   She
had tried many ways of lightening the
depression.   She would read until her
brain was exhausted, or she would practice
or take up her wood-carving, until her
hands refused any longer to work.   Such
thoughts as those just set down only
visited her on these occasions, and then she
could not free herself from their influence.

Then she leaned forward, and, resting her chin on her hand, brooded over the thought of what her loneliness would be when her tutor should be gone. She was so lost in thought that she did not hear him enter the room, and she started when she heard his voice saying—

"What gloomy thoughts can authorize such a gloomy face as that?"

She turned round quickly.

"What were you thinking of?" he inquired.

"I was thinking how desolate this room will look when all your things are gone."

"Chut! you must not think of that. Besides, yours will go at the same time," he said. "Remember, you will live downstairs and be mistress of this house."

"True," she said, and a cloud passed

over her face. The anticipation was evidently unpleasant.

" Will this dispel the gloom ? " asked Philip, after he had looked at her gravely for a few moments ; and he laid before her an open letter and five golden sovereigns.

" What is this ? " asked Margaret, in surprise.

" Read the letter, and you will see."

She took up the letter and read it through ; then she laid it down, and drew a deep breath, while she touched the sovereigns with the tips of her fingers.

" They are mine ?   I have earned them ? " she eagerly asked.

Philip laughed.   " How do you like the letter ? "

"It is delightful.   I shall always keep it. '

It was a letter from the dealer in London.

He had kept Margaret's carvings, and had forwarded an order for five pounds in payment. He said that he had found a ready market for the things, and that he should always be glad to do business with Mr. Welford's friend.

"Now," said Philip, "should the need for it ever come, you may support yourself in two ways. You may begin life either as a milliner and dressmaker, or as a carpenter."

"I have not sold any of my hats and dresses yet," said the girl, laughing. A moment was sufficient to wrap her in complete gloom; a moment was sufficient to bring back the sunshine to her.

"Now," said Philip again, "put all that away, and let us have some reading. You must not try your eyes by carving by lamplight."

She rose and put away her tools, remarking—

"I wonder what Mr. Terry would say if he knew that I have just earned five pounds."

"I am afraid," said Philip, cheerfully, "that he would be very much shocked."

"Any honest employment seems to shock him."

"When you begin to live with him, Margaret, I think you should try to call him by his proper name. He is your grandfather."

"Oh no," she said, quickly. "I shall never be able to call him anything but Mr. Terry; it would not sound natural."

"It is your turn to read," said Philip.

*   *   *   *   *

After that, the time seemed to go very quickly. Margaret felt the weeks flying past sometimes with a sense almost of terror. Her grandfather had decided that she had now power and experience enough to enable her to tread her path through the world alone; or rather, if he had thought about the matter at all, his thoughts would probably have taken that direction. She knew herself very inexperienced, but she could only acquiesce in the arrangement; she was powerless to change anything.

August, September, and October were gone, and "in the gloom of the cloudy November" Philip left Ash Fell. Margaret went with him to the station, and though her face was very pale, she shed no tears as she received his farewell kiss, and watched the train steam out of the little station.

She walked home slowly. She felt terribly sad, and she knew she would have to bear her sadness alone. When she reached her sitting-room, she dropped into a chair and looked yearningly round. The room looked so empty and desolate, she could not bear the sight, and went away to take off her walking things. She had to pass Philip's room. The door stood wide open; two housemaids were dismantling the room. Margaret had borne the parting bravely, but the trivial sight of the disordered furniture seemed to bring straight home the loss she had sustained. Going hastily forward to her own room, she pushed to the door behind her, and, falling on her knees by the bedside, sobbed as if her heart would break.

When she returned to the sitting-room, she sat down by her work-table and, leaning her head in her hands, gave herself up to the contemplation of her own situation.

What was going to happen to her now? Was she to continue to inhabit this room alone, or was she going to live with her grandfather? Her heart beat with a little excitement and nervousness. She did not know what she was to do. Perhaps Mr. Terry had forgotten her existence; ought she to remind him of her presence in the house. She felt that her position was an awkward one, and she hardly knew how to act. She did not want to live with her grandfather, but at the same time she felt it would be very dreary to live in perfect solitude. At last she came to the conclusion that she would do nothing. What indeed could she do? She would wait and see what Mr. Terry did. It was surely for him to decide and to make the first move.

Her early dinner was served at the usual hour. It was the first meal she had eaten alone for a long time, and the experience was so unpleasant that she curtailed it as much as possible. Morris, who had occupied the post of schoolroom maid ever since Margaret had come to Ash Fell, observed the girl's pale cheeks and sad face, and thought to cheer her by remarking that " Miss Terry would find it lonesome at first without Mr. Welford, but life was made up of such troubles, and it did not do to think of them too much."

Margaret could not help smiling, and Morris went away convinced that she had considerably lightened the young lady's heaviness.

About four o'clock, as Margaret sat by the fire reading, Morris appeared with a message from her master, to the effect that he wished to see Miss Terry in the drawing-room at half-past seven that evening.

Margaret received the message with composure. She knew the squire dined at six; when he had dined, then, and slept his evening nap, she was to appear for inspection.

"Perhaps," she thought, "he will find he dislikes me so much that he will send me up here again."

Shortly before half-past seven she went to her room, and exchanged the short, dark morning dress she wore for a long one of cream-coloured cashmere. She wore no jewelry, because she possessed none, not even a locket; only a plain gold brooch which had belonged to her mother. Thus dressed, she looked what she was, a very beautiful and a very proud English girl.

Mr. Terry was alone when Margaret entered the drawing-room. He was sitting in front of the fire, but turned at the sound of the opening door, and then rose, uncertain how to greet the girl. He had arranged a greeting in his mind, but it was intended for a girl who should enter the room awkwardly, and be shy and nervous, and very possibly badly dressed. It struck even him as inapplicable to this dignified, self-possessed young lady, who was dressed with the simple quiet taste of a gentle-woman, and who walked forward as though entering her own drawing-room. Being thrown off the track he had prescribed for himself, he was for a moment embarrassed, and said nothing. Margaret, to whom this silence was rather disagreeable, broke it by saying courteously—

"Good evening."

"Good evening, Miss Terry," replied the old man, recovering himself. Then he wheeled forward a low chair for her, and she seated herself serenely in front of the fire.

The squire remained standing, and he looked at Margaret coldly. She did not seem to notice it; she was looking at a picture which hung over the mantelpiece. It was an original Landseer, and being passionately fond of animals, she thought it very beautiful. Her attention was called from it by hearing her grandfather speak.

"I sent for you to-night to speak about your future life."

"Yes," she said quietly, turning her face to his.

"You have finished your education; you are a young woman. I believe you are seventeen."

"I am eighteen," she said, looking straight at him.

For a moment Mr. Terry was silent.

Margaret's words brought back to his mind, as doubtless they did to her own, a scene which had taken place some four years before. Some old friends of Mr. Terry's had called. They had heard of his adoption of what they called " poor Eustace's child," and asked to see her. Mr. Terry would fain have said she was out, but at that moment she crossed the lawn in front of the window, and he had to ring the bell and request her presence. She came in, a tall, beautiful girl of fourteen, with "fearless eyes and grey," which looked frankly in the faces of the assembled party. The squire saw her, and, with a nod in the direction where she stood, said—

" There is my granddaughter, Mrs. Main-waring."

" Ah !" said the lady, turning to the girl, " she is not like poor Eustace. What is her name ? "

There was the slightest possible pause, and then the squire said boldly—

"Edith."

Margaret's face had flushed hotly. Her grandfather had forgotten her name.

She looked straight at him, and said decisively—

"My name is Margaret, not Edith."

She was very soon sent away, but she had never either forgotten or forgiven the circumstance, and the recollection of it was probably in the minds of both when she said to her grandfather—

"I am eighteen."

"Eighteen, then," he said, after a moment's silence. "Mrs. Entwistle thinks you are old enough to be introduced into society. You will live with me now, and sit at my table. Mrs. Fenton will give up her keys to you; you will be mistress here,"

"Am I to keep the housekeeping money?" she asked.

It was a simple enough question, yet it seemed to excite the squire strangely. His eyebrows lowered, and his face darkened.

"What do you mean?" he asked, looking down upon the girl, who had taken a hand-screen from the mantelpiece and now held it carelessly between her face and the blaze.

"Only," she answered, "that all the money you let me spend before, you did not allow me to keep myself. I thought perhaps you could not trust me yet."

"Understand once for all," he said, almost savagely, "that I want to have no more to do with you than I am obliged. I am at present obliged to occupy the same rooms with you, but it will only be until you are married, and the sooner that happens the better for you."

She looked up into his face; she was not in the least frightened of this fierce old man.

"Thank you for telling me all this; it is much better to know how we are to go on."

Later in the evening Mrs. Entwistle and her nephew, the curate, dropped in. Mrs. Entwistle smiled upon the girl, and then withdrew into the background with the squire, leaving Margaret to the care of her nephew.

The Rev. Adolphe Entwistle was a young man of medium height, and slender proportions. Margaret knew him by sight, but had never spoken to him. He had a fair complexion, and the highly arched eyebrows which always give an expression of distress and timidity to a face. He was six or seven and twenty years of age, and had not been at Ash Fell more than twelve months,

Before his ordination he had been a master at a large grammar school, and had then worn a moustache. On taking orders he had abolished it. Margaret did not know that; but she wondered, with a kind of indifferent wonder, what infatuation had led him to expose the pitiful weakness of his mouth and chin.

The Rev. Adolphe, however, began to talk to her, and she was forced to listen.

"I suppose now, Miss Terry, you will take a prominent part in our parish matters. We are sorely in need of a helping hand, and will give you a warm welcome."

"I do not think parish matters interest me," she said, indifferently.

"I cannot imagine a young lady not taking an interest in her parish."

"I know very little about such things."

"You will, at any rate, relieve my aunt

of the burden of the choir duty. She is both organist and choir-mistress at present."

"I am afraid I can hardly be of use to Mrs. Entwistle. I cannot sing, and I never learnt to play the organ."

"My aunt can soon teach you," he said, eagerly.

"You are very good, to make such liberal promises for her; but I could not allow myself to impose another burden on Mrs. Entwistle, when she has already so many."

She smiled as she spoke with a kind of cold malice, and the curate bit his lip. He was not accustomed to have his own words turned against him.

In this way the evening wore on. The Rev. Adolphe hardly left Margaret's side, but kept up an unceasing stream of small talk, which wearied her, unused as she was to that style of conversation. She grew very tired of her companion, and heartily wished that he would leave her.

Meanwhile, Mrs. Entwistle was "taking stock" of Margaret. She eyed her over from the crown of her golden head to the tip of the slender, satin-slippered foot, resting so lightly on the quaint, old-fashioned footstool; and as she looked she felt half-jealous and half-pleased, for she had her project, though as yet she had confided it to no one.

She got a few words with the girl before they parted.

"I hear you are going to depose Mrs. Fenton," she said, with ponderous playfulness. "Of course you will be all at sea at first, but you must always come to me in your difficulties. I have not forgotten my first attempts at housekeeping."

"Thank you," said Margaret; "but I

think I shall manage. I used to spend two days a week with Mrs. Fenton, learning housekeeping."

" Indeed ! Was that Mr. Welford's wish or your own ?"

" Mr. Welford's. I did not care about it."

Soon after they were gone, Margaret went upstairs. She sat thinking for a long time before undressing. How wearisome the curate had been ! She hoped she should not see him often. Then she thought of what her grandfather had said, and her lips closed firmly together. If he counted on her speedy marriage with any one who asked for her, as an easy mode of getting rid of her, he would find he did not know with whom he had to deal.

CHAPTER VII.

" The story of her life from day to day."

MARGARET's life was a very regular and a
very quiet one. She saw very little of
Mr. Terry : they seldom met except at
meals, and then but little conversation
passed between them. Neither, to her
great relief, did she see so much of Mrs.
Entwistle as she had expected to do. The
only person she did see often was the
Rev. Adolphe, and she seldom passed a
day without meeting him. Either he
called with a message from his aunt, or
she went into the garden, and found him
walking there with Mr. Terry. If she

rode or drove, she was certain to meet him ; and, as he always behaved in such a way that to pass by without speaking would have involved absolute discourtesy on her part, she spoke to him nearly every day too.

She had regarded him at first with indifference ; but her indifference could not last long. She began actively to dislike him, and when she mentioned him in her letters to Philip, it was under the name of "my pet aversion." She wondered sometimes if he knew how she disliked him, for she did not trouble to conceal her feelings. In her house she treated him of necessity with courtesy, but out of doors her manners were uniformly cold and distant.

At the same time, her new life was not an unhappy one. Though she was lonely,

Philip's letters served to enliven her. She received them regularly, and they were ever a new delight to her. However delightful was the expectation she formed of each one, the reality was sure to surpass the anticipation. He told her a great deal of his life, and, among other things, that he no longer lived in his mother's house. Another letter contained the news of the death of his Aunt Margaret. She, in her turn, sent him a detailed account of how she spent her time. They had been too long together, and knew each other too well, for such details ever to become wearisome or devoid of interest.

She was free to spend her days as she choose; her grandfather was too indifferent to her to care how she employed her time. Her favourite books remained to her, as also her wood-carving, and other exercises.

She had ordered that the old sitting-room should remain as she and Philip had left it, and she spent much time there over her carving. She also spent hours in the large bare room, with the great swing windows, which were always open. The room was at the top of the house, and Philip had had it fitted up as a gymnasium for her.

The introduction into society which had been so much insisted upon on her emancipation from the schoolroom, had never taken place. It was now the middle of January, and as yet she had seen little more society than when she had lived with Philip. About this time, however, her grandfather told her he was going to have some friends to dinner.

" How many people will there be ? " she asked.

" Six, and with ourselves and Entwistle
and his wife and nephew we shall be a
dozen.   Larger parties are a mistake."

" Who are the people ? "

" All men, friends of mine."

Margaret was silent; then she said—

" Why is Mrs. Entwistle coming, if it
is to be a man's party ?   I have to be here,
but I do not see—— "

The squire interrupted her sharply.

" I ask whom I please to dine at my
own table.   Mrs. Entwistle is like my own
daughter, as she would have been if your
father had not been the greatest fool that
ever lived, and your mother—— "   He
paused, arrested by the look in her face;
then he went on hastily, " I also wish
there should be a lady present to show you
how to behave.   I do not choose that you
should disgrace yourself before my friends."

"I think I know how to behave," she said, coldly. "I was brought up by a gentleman, whatever my future associates may be."

On the evening of the dinner-party Mrs. Entwistle came early. It was her privilege to behave as though Ash Fell Hall were her home, and she fully availed herself of it. This evening she was so early that Margaret had only just come down to the drawing-room, and was warming her hands at the fire. She was dressed almost as simply as on the evening when she first sat in the drawing-room. Her dress was white. She wore deep red chrysanthemums in her hair and at her throat; they were her only ornaments.

Mrs. Entwistle scanned her narrowly. She herself was gorgeously attired; she was fond of rich silks and brilliant colours. Having completed her survey, she said—

"I have always forgotten to ask who your dressmaker is, Margaret; she suits you perfectly."

"I make my dresses myself."

"You are very clever. They would do credit to a professional. Imagine"—turning to the squire, who just then came in—"Margaret makes her own dresses! Who taught you?"

"Mr. Welford engaged a dressmaker who came here. She taught me millinery and dressmaking."

"This Mr. Welford seems to have been a *rara avis*," said Agatha, with a laugh that was half a sneer. "One does not generally expect to find tutors who teach dressmaking. But see, Margaret has no jewelry. It is absurd to see a girl in her position without a scrap of jewelry. That little brooch is too plain for a dinner-party. Where did you get it? It is old-fashioned, but there is something quaint and uncommon about it."

Margaret involuntarily put her hand to her throat.

"I always wear it," she said. "It belonged to my mother."

Describing the scene a few days later in a letter to Philip, she said—

"Mr. Terry looked as if he would have liked to tear the brooch from my dress, and crush it under his foot."

As a matter of course, he did nothing of the kind, but said contemptuously—

"You are right, Agatha."

Before Margaret had time to reply, the first guest was announced, and the conversation could be carried on no further.

The dinner passed off well, though the squire saw with vexation that it was Margaret who rose first, and Mrs. Entwistle who followed her example.

The circumstance made him ask himself whether an inflexible will was not one of the qualities Margaret had inherited from her mother.

" I must get her married before long," he thought. " If she is going to oppose me, I shall never stand it."

Alone with Margaret in the drawing-room, Mrs. Entwistle asked the girl what she thought of her nephew, the Rev. Adolphe.

" I never think about him at all," said Margaret, indifferently.

" How is that ? "

" We only think of people and things that strike us as being in some way interesting. Mr. Entwistle does not interest me in any way."

"He is a very good young man," remarked his aunt, almost to herself.

"In what way?" asked Margaret, with polite indifference.

"How can you ask? When did you ever hear of Adolphe doing anything wicked?"

Margaret smiled. "Goodness, I think, consists less in passive abstaining from evil than in being actively useful and good."

"Well," said Mrs. Entwistle, rather sharply, "Adolphe is 'actively useful and good,' as you call it, too. He is most active in the parish, and a most zealous worker for the Church."

Again Margaret smiled, though this time she said nothing.

Mrs. Entwistle did not seem to like the girl's silence. She fidgeted in her chair,

turned over the leaves of a photograph
album, then closed the book and pushed it
from her; finally, she said—

"You don't make such a friend of
Adolphe as I had hoped you would."

"Why should I make a friend of him ? "

"Why ? You must sometimes want a
friend and adviser."

"Mr. Welford is my friend and adviser."

"But he is not here. Do you never
want instant advice, advice which only a
clergyman can give ? "

The colour came into Margaret's face.
She was innocent beyond the ordinary run
of girls, but she was certainly not stupid.
The constant presence of Mr. Entwistle,
and the continual mention of his name, and
laudation of himself when he was not present, which she had hitherto regarded as
infatuation on the part of the young man's

relatives, suddenly appeared to her in a new light, and she said rather haughtily—

" This is a strange subject of conversation to choose, but I am not so dependent upon other people as you seem to imagine. Mr. Welford taught me to think and judge for myself."

She felt angry, and she was not a woman who used blunted weapons to fence with.

Soon after this the men came in, and Margaret was immediately pounced upon by her " pet aversion." This evening she felt utterly unable to endure his society, and was very glad when another man came up and joined them.

The new-comer had taken her into dinner, and they had had much conversation together. They had been talking about a book on manners and customs in Japan, which had just come out, and which

Margaret had been reading with great interest. Mr. Barton continued to speak on the same subject; he knew the author of the book, and was giving Margaret some interesting details respecting his private life. They took but little notice of the Rev. Adolphe, and he grew more and more sulky as he noticed how completely Margaret's attention was withdrawn from him. At last he rose abruptly, saying—

" I cannot understand what interest you find in such subjects, Miss Terry. Had it been anything connected with the parish here, or even with some missionary society in India, or one of those countries, I could better have comprehended your enthusiasm; as it is, I fail to account for your interest in a semi-barbarous people such as the Japanese."

" Semi-barbarous ! " echoed Margaret, in

some doubt as to whether she had heard correctly. " If that is your idea, I need not ask if you have read this book."

" Certainly not; such books possess but slight interest for me. I confess I have enough to interest me at home ; I know very little about the Japanese, and care less."

Margaret looked at him for a moment, and then turned to her companion, who had been watching the scene with an amused smile, and said, while her lips curled contemptuously—

" He knows nothing. Don't you wonder how any one *dare* be so ignorant ? "

Every word dropped clearly from her lips, and though the curate had moved away to some little distance, it was plainly to be seen, from the expression on the reverend gentleman's face, that he had heard her speech.

Mr. Barton laughed, half with amusement, half with contempt, as he replied—

" Oh, you must not be too hard on him. Young men of the present day seem to have lost the taste or the power of reading and acquiring knowledge."

The following day, when the Rev. Adolphe called at the Vicarage, he was in a very bad temper. His aunt received him alone. She had witnessed the scene in the drawing-room on the previous evening, and was displeased with her nephew.

" I am angry with you," she said, as sharply as she ever spoke to him. " If you obey my instructions so poorly, I shall refuse to help you at all. What possessed you to behave as you did to Margaret last night ? "

The Rev. Adolphe played with his hat, and looked supremely sulky.

"I don't know what you mean," he said.

"Then, you are very dense. Why do you always behave as though she were better than yourself? A girl of her character likes a man who shows that he is going to be her master. Until you take a more high-handed tone you will never make any progress. You talk too much about the parish and local matters; that is another mistake."

"What else can I talk about?" he asked, half impatiently.

"What indeed!" she might have said, but she went on. "She is one of those girls who fancy they like literary men, and who go in for 'mind.' To gain her good-will, you must talk about books and politics and public questions."

But here the curate rebelled.

"Nay," he said, "I cannot do that."

She laughed and shrugged her shoulders.

" Then, my dear boy, you must make up your mind to see her and her future fifteen thousand a year bestowed on some one else."

The young man was silent for some time ; then he went on—

" I have her grandfather's consent to win her ; surely she will not disobey him ? "

" You think not ?   You are grievously mistaken.   Margaret is one of those women who will yield nine points of the law without a word, perhaps for the sake of peace, or because she holds them of but little consequence ; but she will cling to the tenth with all her strength.   If her grandfather tells her to give up rowing or not to ride out without a groom, she will obey him ; but if he tries to marry her to a man she does not like, she will look him straight in the face with her great calm eyes, and refuse point blank to obey him."

"Do you know," he said, with a half laugh, "that you are not describing a particularly agreeable wife? How if, when we are married, she should be willing to do everything else, but should refuse to give up corresponding with that Welford?"

"How do you know she corresponds with him?"

Mrs. Entwistle looked thoughtful; then she said—

"Come, Adolphe, you must not despair because you find a little difficulty at first. Few men in your position have so good a chance of marrying such a fortune as Margaret will have sometime. Go now, I am busy, but remember what I have said, and try to act upon it. A woman understands another woman far better than a man does, believe me."

The curate went away, hardly knowing whether he should feel elated or depressed.

A week or two after the dinner-party, Mr. Terry had given Margaret a parcel, saying she would find some ornaments in it which he desired she would wear whenever they had any guests. Mrs. Entwistle, he said, had chosen them, so they will sure to be right.

Margaret took the parcel, merely saying, "Thank you." She put it aside and went on with her work, only taking it up again when she went to bed.

Alone in her room, she opened the parcel, and found it to contain several cases. These she opened, and spread the contents upon the dressing-table.

"They are for 'Miss Terry,' not for me,"

she thought as she looked at the ornaments. " I have a certain appearance to keep up as his granddaughter, otherwise he would give me nothing. He will never let me have the Terry emeralds. All of the best," she continued, turning over the things with a sneer which suited her beautiful face but ill.

She put the ornaments on. There were earrings, which she tossed contemptuously aside however, two bracelets, a brooch, and necklace. When she had hung them on, she looked at herself in a mirror. " I look like a third-rate actress," she murmured, half aloud. Then she took them off, thinking, " They must have cost a great deal of money, but they were for Miss Terry, not for me."

CHAPTER VIII.

" Go to! I hate this humble-minded pride,
Self-willed submission to your own pert fancies ;
This fog-bed, mushroom spawn, of brain-sick wits,
Who make their oddities their test for grace.
I . . .
Do otherwise conceive of love. Farewell."

MEANWHILE, the Rev. Adolphe's wooing
made but little progress. Margaret was no
more hostile to him than she had ever
been. She had exhausted him, and her
feelings remained unchanged. He bored
her as much as before, but she had lately
begun to treat him with less ceremony,
and left him alone when she could endure
his society no longer. She knew why he

haunted her so persistently, but she trusted
that if she preserved her present frigid
attitude, and never gave him any opportunity of speaking on the subject, he could
not but see that his suit was unwelcome,
and would retire like a gentleman. She
sadly deceived herself. The more she en-
trenched herself behind a haughty reserve,
the more persuasive and fascinating became
Mr. Entwistle's manner. He had per-
suaded himself that he was in love with
Margaret, and as it was impossible his
affections should be bestowed upon an un-
responsive object, it naturally followed that
she must love him. Still, he had not the
courage to put his fortune to the test, and
he delayed so long that Mrs. Entwistle was
in a fever of excitement and apprehension.

Margaret's relations with her grandfather
were unchanged. She was coldly polite,

and fulfilled perfectly her duties as mistress of the house; he was silent, morose, and contemptuous. He seldom spoke to her, and never betrayed any interest or concern in anything she did or said. She was therefore surprised when, one afternoon as she sat in the library writing to Philip, the squire, coming in, looked at her suspiciously. He inquired if she had seen some book he appeared to be seeking, and on her replying in the negative and turning again to her letter, he asked abruptly—

" To whom are you writing ? "

" To Mr. Welford," she answered, her surprise visible on her face.

" Are you in the habit of writing to him ? "

" Yes."

" You will cease writing to him at once.

" Why am I to give it up ? "

Her voice was cold. It irritated him, and he went on—

"I should have thought that even you would have known that a girl does not correspond with one man when she is going to marry another."

Margaret's heart gave a great leap, but she went on quietly—

"Even if I were engaged, I should not see any reason for breaking off my correspondence with Mr. Welford; but I am not going to be married—nothing is further from my intention."

"Perhaps not; but your intentions will not be consulted. I have arranged a marriage for you perfectly suitable in every way, and all you have to do is to acquiesce in it."

"Which I never shall do," she answered, promptly. Then, more quietly, she went on, " And who is the man who submits to have his wooing done for him ? "

" Adolphe Entwistle."

" And you call that a suitable match for me ? " scornfully.

She had risen, and was standing before him, looking straight into his face with " her great calm eyes," as Mrs. Entwistle had foretold. The squire was not above middle height ; Margaret was a tall woman, and she stood with her face on a level with his. She was perfectly cool, and that fact only served to lash him into a greater rage than before.

" If I had spoken the truth," he said, brutally, " I should have said he was much too good for you. His father was a gentleman against whom nothing has ever been said, and his mother is a lady of title ; while your—— "

He paused, choked with anger. She went on with simple dignity—

"My father was a gentleman too, and my mother was a pure and high-minded woman. The highest lady in the land can be no more than that."

"He is your superior in every way," he went on, excitedly.

She smiled without speaking, half in derision, half in contempt, and the squire repeated wrathfully—

"You shall marry him."

"You seem to have settled all this in your mind," she said. "May I ask if you have spoken of it to Mr. Entwistle?"

"Certainly."

"Then you had better tell him at once, that the sooner he rids his mind of such folly the better; he cannot have the slightest hope of success."

" What do you mean ? " he asked, staggered by her perfect self-possession and determination.

" That I will not marry Mr. Entwistle, or any other man."

" You will do as you are told."

" On so important a question as marriage I shall consult my own inclinations. I shall marry at no one's bidding, and for no one's pleasure but my own. And now let us consider the matter as settled."

" It is nothing less than settled," he cried inconsistently; and he would doubtless have proceeded to excite himself further had not a footman appeared upon the scene, with a message which obliged Mr. Terry to hurry away.

The old footman had been at the door for some time before he had been seen, and Margaret's last speech had reached his ears.

He had, unnoticed, eyed her with approval, and as he went away he thought—

"She's a rare spirit of her own ; ay, and she'll want it all in this world too. She'll meet him on his own ground, and fight as hard as he will, and I doubt it'll go hard but she'll beat him too."

Left alone, Margaret resumed her seat at the writing-table, and, leaning her chin on her hands, looked out of the window, across the garden, gay with spring flowers, to where the moor shut in the prospect. Even now she was calm, except when she thought of the look on the squire's face when he had spoken of her mother, and then her grey eyes flashed with anger. But she had said that she would not marry Adolphe Entwistle, and with her the matter was ended. She was one of those women who, having once made up their minds to

act as they deem right, can dismiss the
disputed point from their thoughts, for
they know that no consideration will make
them swerve from their decision. Now,
therefore, as she sat looking gravely from
the window, she was not thinking of how
to defend her position, or trying to find
new arguments behind which to entrench
herself, but of the end of the sentence she
had half written when the squire burst in
upon her solitude. When she had found
it she took up her pen again, and returned
to her letter with a mind untroubled by
gloomy forebodings.

Several days passed, during which Margaret heard nothing of Mr. Entwistle. He
did not come to the house, and when his
presence was withdrawn he ceased to
occupy any place in her thoughts. Mr.
Terry did not address her; she was abso-

lutely alone. She enjoyed her solitude.
She spent her mornings in walking and
riding, and many hours at her work-table.
She had written to Philip on the subject,
and received a prompt reply to her letter.
He told her that he did not suppose she
was in any danger of yielding, but if such
a thought should have occurred to her, he
prayed her not to let her resolution falter.
It would be madness and intellectual
suicide for her to marry such a man.

This letter, though it had cheered Margaret, made her smile. The idea of yielding
was so far from her that Philip's warning,
even though she knew he did not suspect
her of unsteadiness of purpose, caused
her a little amusement.

Sometimes she asked herself why she
stayed at Ash Fell, when she knew she
could support herself whenever she chose

to leave her grandfather's house.   But she
shrank from taking such a step.   She
knew she was her grandfather's heiress,
and, though she neither loved money nor
cared for the position she would occupy as
mistress of Ash Fell Hall, she still wished
to have that position.   Her heart swelled
with anger and her cheeks grew hot with
shame often, as she rode through the
village and saw the state in which many of
the people lived.   Mr. Terry was a hard
man, and cared little how his tenants were
lodged, so long as they paid their rents
and had anything like a roof over their
heads.

Only once had Margaret been moved to
address her grandfather on any other
subject than those she was obliged to dis-
cuss.   She had appealed to him on behalf
of a man, who had been caught in some

misdemeanour, and, having been sentenced
to prison, was in great anxiety about
leaving his wife and children. She had
begged Mr. Terry to show mercy, but in
vain. She had been told roughly to mind
her own business, and not to meddle with
things she did not understand. She had
obeyed him, and the subject had never
again been mentioned.

Some ten days had gone by since she
had been forbidden to write to Philip,
when Margaret was suddenly reminded of
the existence of the Rev. Adolphe Entwistle
by his reappearance at the Hall. He came
upon her one afternoon as she sat reading
under the huge copper beech on the lawn.
She was feeling very content. Her book
interested her, and the afternoon was so
beautiful it seemed happiness enough
merely to exist. A cloud passed over her

face as the curate came up, but she returned his greeting with the same quiet courtesy she had ever shown him.

He drew up one of the wicker garden-chairs to her side, and, seating himself, began to talk to her. The conversation might almost have been called a monologue, it was so completely on one side, her answers to his questions being of the briefest description. She half guessed on what errand he had come, for his manner was nervous and hesitating, though it occasionally grew warmer, as if he would advance to a greater degree of familiarity. She, however, never wavered from her attitude of calm, even politeness, which he must have felt to be unfavourable to him. Presently there came a pause, which lasted so long that Margaret began to steal glances at her open book, and had even read through a paragraph, when Mr. Entwistle suddenly spoke again. This time it was to ask her to be his wife.

Margaret heard him in silence—an ominous silence, surely, for she continued to lean back in her chair and to watch the two dogs playing on the lawn close by, neither did her face show any confusion. When he had finished she did not speak immediately, and the curate could hear his heart beat as he waited for her answer.

"From what you have said, Mr. Entwistle, it seems that you have spoken to Mr. Terry on this subject."

"Certainly. I did not feel at liberty to address myself to you until he had given me his consent, and, I may add, his best wishes for my success."

"When was the subject last mentioned between you?" she asked, a little curiously.

" Yesterday evening."

" Did he lead you to suppose then that I should give you a favourable answer ? "

" Certainly," in some surprise; and she did him the justice to detect the ring of truth in his voice. " Why should he have changed his mind ? " he went on.

" He deceived you," she said quietly. " Ten days ago he told me of your intention, and I asked him to tell you to rid your mind of such folly at once."

The curate flushed hotly with mortification.

" What do you mean ? " he asked.

" We cannot marry," she said, gravely. " We have nothing in common; we have never been friends. From what you have said this afternoon, I imagine that my ideas of love and marriage are very different from yours. It would be impossible for us to marry."

The curate was silent. Such a refusal seemed decided enough; he could not put down such words as she had just used entirely to maiden coyness, which would yield on gentle pressure. And yet the thought that he had failed was intolerable to him. He thought of the squire, who expected him to rid him of an uncongenial burden; of Mrs. Entwistle, whose eyes were fixed upon the future, bright with a golden harvest for her nephew, and he felt he dare not face these two and tell them he had failed.

" Are you not answering rather hastily?" he pleaded. " Are you so rich in friends that you can afford to throw my love lightly away? "

She flushed as he spoke. She had not

intended that he should know her candid opinion of him, but since he would not take his answer, let the consequences be upon his own head.

" Your love ? " she said slowly, and a little contemptuously. " Do you love me, or the money I may one day have, Mr. Entwistle ? I said just now that our ideas of love and marriage were different. I had not intended to speak more plainly, but you force me to do so. If I ever marry, I hope my husband will be willing to take me for my own sake, not for that of my fortune. Good afternoon."

She turned to her book without trying to hide her purpose now, and Mr. Entwistle took the hint and departed, sore at heart; while she remained cool and composed in her place, and resumed her reading almost before he had reached the gravel path which bounded the lawn.

So quiet and unemotional had been the scene between them, that, though two gardeners were at work not a hundred yards from the copper beech, they had not the slightest idea of what was taking place so near them.

Margaret felt certain that her grandfather would open the vials of his wrath upon her that evening; but though he looked rather more unamiable than usual, he did not mention Mr. Entwistle's name. She was surprised, but said nothing. She had requested that the subject should not be mentioned again, and after that could not herself introduce it.

The next day passed in silence, and the next. The days went on until a week had gone by, and still the squire made no sign. His silence rather worried Margaret. She knew him too well to suppose that he would let the matter drop without making any allusion to it, and she wished impatiently that, if he were going to speak, he would do so at once.

She had not much longer to wait. A day or two later, the squire came to dinner with a face even darker than usual. She boded no good from the fact, and when he followed her to the drawing-room some half-hour after she had left him alone, and, seating himself in his armchair, glared fiercely at her, she knew her hour was come. She was working, delicately embroidering a cambric handkerchief, when his voice sounded through the room.

" Put down that work, and listen to me."

She did as she was desired, and he went on—

" What is this I hear from young Entwistle ? "

" Yes," she answered.

" Don't trifle with me, I won't stand it. Did he make you an offer of marriage last week ? "

" Yes."

" And you declined it ? "

" Yes, I declined it."

" For what reason ? "

" I had no wish to marry him."

" In spite of what I said to you some time ago ? "

" I told you then I would not marry him ; you cannot have forgotten."

" I have not forgotten, but I lay very little weight upon your reasoning and your words. I have said you shall marry Adolphe Entwistle, and you shall."

" I will not marry him," she said, firmly.

" Do you refuse to obey me ? "

" In this case, yes. I will obey you in

anything else. I do not know that I have
ever wished to displease you before, but in
this case I claim the right to act according
to my own judgment."

"You claim! you claim!" he cried,
furious with rage, and maddened by her
calm opposition. "I should like to know
what right you have to claim anything!
A penniless beggar brat that I picked out
of the gutter, and took into my own house.
I should like to know what such as you can
lay claim to! I hate your hypocrisy. So
long as it will serve your turn you will
obey me, and think to cast off your obedience
when it clashes with your inclinations.
You think you can lay claim to anything,
do you, when every penny you spend,
every morsel you eat, everything you wear,
has been given you by me. You are
dependent on me for the very air you

breathe, and if I were to cast you off you would fall back to the beggary from which I took you."

"No," she said, suddenly raising her head, for his torrent of words had overwhelmed and stunned her. "I am not dependent on you; I am independent. Do you think Mr. Welford never guessed that such a day as this would come, or that he left me without preparation for it? He taught me how to earn my living. If I left your house to-night I could work."

"Work!" he cried, with an accent of the deepest scorn. "I should like to see you work. You have as much inclination to work as your mother, who fooled my poor lad into marrying her, and thought to be mistress of this house; but—— "

"Stop!" she cried, her voice ringing

through the room. "This discussion does not touch my mother; be good enough to leave her name out. If you say one more insulting word of her I will leave your house to-morrow."

His face took an expression of fiendish malignity. He looked at her furiously. Had she shown the least sign of fear, he would probably have struck her; but she had never been taught to think that a graceful timidity is becoming in a woman, and she stood firm and unblenching before him. He did not dare to strike her, but looked at her for a moment with all his hatred of her visible in his face; then suddenly his face changed, his arm dropped nerveless to his side, and he fell insensible to the ground.

The girl's first feeling was of sheer terror, but she did not lose her self-possession. Her grandfather had hardly fallen before she was kneeling at his side, after having rung the bell.

In her agitation she had rung the bell violently, and the old footman answered the summons without delay. He could not repress a cry of horror at the sight before him, and Margaret said quickly—

"Mr. Terry has had a fit. You must send one of the grooms directly for Dr. Hunter, and then come back and help me to lift him on to the couch."

In a few minutes the old man had done her bidding, and was with her again. Together they lifted the squire on to the couch, and Margaret applied all kinds of restoratives, but in vain; the heavy eyelids were not lifted, nor did the tightly shut lips unclose. The girl began to think the doctor would never come, and it seemed an eternity, though in reality it was but half an hour, before she heard the grating of his carriage-wheels on the gravel outside.

She rose from her kneeling position as he entered the room, and held out her hand.

" I am so glad you are here, Dr. Hunter."

" My dear Miss Terry, this is very shocking. When did it happen ? "

" About half an hour ago," she answered, looking mechanically at the clock.

Mr. Terry's man was present, and by Dr. Hunter's directions Mr. Terry was carried upstairs and put to bed.

Margaret was left alone in the drawing-room, standing, with fast-beating heart, looking from one of the windows. She had not been there long when Mrs. Entwistle was announced.

"My dear Margaret," said the lady, hurrying to the girl's side, "how terrible this is! When did it happen?"

"How did you hear of it?"

"I met the groom as he was coming back from Dr. Hunter's, and, of course, came here at once. Where is your grandfather now?"

"In his room. Dr. Hunter is with him. I expect he will come down before long to tell me what he thinks of him."

"Were you alone with him when it happened?"

"Yes."

"Really, Margaret," wiping her eyes, "how coldly you speak! One would imagine that you did not care whether your grandfather lived or died."

Margaret made no answer, she felt as if in a dream. At that moment Dr. Hunter came in. He seemed surprised to see Mrs. Entwistle, and, after returning her greeting and answering one or two of her questions about Mr. Terry, he addressed himself exclusively to Margaret.

" Your grandfather is conscious now, though I cannot say how long he will remain so. It was an apoplectic fit; the second shock may follow in a few days, or not for weeks, or even months. He is quiet, and does not seem to wish to see anybody." This was intended for Mrs. Entwistle.

" I understand," said Margaret. " I will not go to him at present; I think my presence would disturb him."

" Just as you think best, Miss Terry; but if you do not go yourself, I must request that he sees no one else."

He then gave her a few directions, and

took his leave, saying he would look in again the last thing at night. Soon afterwards Mrs. Entwistle went home.

Of course all question of Margaret's leaving Ash Fell was set at rest. She could not have gone now. Her days were fully occupied. She had to see many people, some complete strangers to her, who came to inquire after Mr. Terry, and she spent a great deal of time in her grandfather's sick-room. He hated her presence, but was too feeble to protest against it; he had, too, a dim feeling that her touch was firmer and more gentle than that of any of his servants. Often, when she went to her room at night, she was too tired to do anything more than undress as quickly as she could and throw herself on her bed.

Her grandfather had suffered a second

shock a few days after the first, but Dr.
Hunter said months would probably elapse
before the third and fatal one would follow.
Sometimes the old man lay in bed perfectly
still for days without speaking; occasionally
he dozed or lay with his eyes shut; but
more frequently they were wide open and
followed Margaret unceasingly as she moved
about the room, or fixed upon her as she
sat by his bedside. At other times he
seemed stronger, and could bear to sit
up in bed and hear the papers read to him.
He seldom spoke to any one, though he
often muttered to himself in a low, indistinct voice. One day, as the doctor was
bending over his patient, he saw that the
old man's eyes were fixed upon Margaret,
who stood at the window, and he heard the
slow muttered words—

"Independent is she? We will see how

far that will go ; I will give her every
chance of keeping up her independence."

So the summer rolled away and passed
into autumn ; dull November, with weeping
skies, clad in grey pall of mist and fog,
held sway over the land, and in November
Mr. Terry died.

The end was very quiet. He had been
sinking gradually for some time, and
Margaret was not surprised when Dr.
Hunter told her one day, that if she thought
there were any people in the village whom
Mr. Terry would like to see round his death-
bed, they should be summoned before night.
She sent to the vicar and his wife, and
then, though with some reluctance, for the
Rev. Adolphe. These people, with Mrs.
Fenton and one or two other old and
faithful servants, stood round Mr. Terry as
he lay dying.

During the last few days of his illness his manner had perceptibly altered. Restless and uneasy, his eyes wandered round the room and rested continually on the figure of his granddaughter. He was powerless to speak, and no one guessed what he wanted. From the feeble signs he made, from the troubled sighs which broke from his lips, no one understood that he had repented of his hardness to Margaret, and would fain have been reconciled with her before he died; Margaret, least of all, expected such a change. So he died with Agatha's hand in his, and with her lips pressed to his forehead.

CHAPTER IX.

> " All my life
> Is open to you.   I go hence
> To London, to the gathering place of souls,
> To live mine straight out."

IT was four days since Mr. Terry's death, and the funeral had just taken place.   A few of the mourners were gathered in the library at the Hall, waiting for the will to be read.   The party consisted of the vicar and his wife, the Rev. Adolphe Entwistle, Margaret, and Mr. Banks, the lawyer.

Margaret was pale, though perfectly composed ; the vicar looked sedately interested ; Mrs. Entwistle and the curate nervously

excited; Mr. Banks was naturally indifferent.

The will was read. Silence had prevailed during the reading of the document;
silence still prevailed when its contents
had been made known. The will, which
had been drawn up during the first days
of Mr. Terry's illness, was so different from
what they had expected. Mrs. Entwistle
and her nephew had speculated no little on
the results of Mr. Terry's death, but their
speculations had never equalled the reality.

Mr. Terry had left half his fortune, with
Ash Fell Hall and its furniture, to his
stepdaughter, Mrs. Latimer, a woman whom
he had always disliked, as everybody knew.
The other half was distributed in legacies;
ten thousand to the Rev. Adolphe, some
very handsome sums to old servants, and
the rest to different people. To Agatha

Entwistle he left the Terry emeralds, than which there were none finer in England. Margaret's name was not mentioned.

Mr. Banks's broke the silence, and his professional voice warmed as he said—

" This is an unjust will, Miss Terry. Had my influence with your grandfather been greater, it would have been different."

Mr. Banks had seen Margaret more than once during his late visits to her grandfather, and each time she had found increasing grace in his eyes.

" It does not signify," she said, absently.

He looked away impatiently, and Mrs. Entwistle and the curate began to exchange congratulations. Mr. Banks turned to the lady, and said—

" This is the first time the emeralds have left the family. I confess, I should hesitate to accept them."

"I am not superstitious," she answered, laughing. "At any rate, I am willing to risk it. Come, Geoffrey and Adolphe, it is high time we went."

Margaret turned to Mr. Banks.

"You will let me give you some lunch before you go," she said. "That is," suddenly becoming alive to the present, "if I may offer hospitality in a house that is no longer my home."

Mr. Banks accepted her offer, adding, "I should like a little conversation with you before I go."

"Ah, Margaret," said Mrs. Entwistle, suddenly recalled to a sense of the girl's presence, "what will you do, you poor child?"

She could not restrain a smile at Mrs. Entwistle's manner.

"You know," went on the lady, patronizingly, " that I shall be glad to see you at my house."

" Thank you; but I will remain here for the present. I dare say Mrs. Latimer would not refuse me if I could ask her permission."

Mrs. Entwistle went away, and Margaret and Mr. Banks were left alone.

" How long will it be before lunch is ready ? " asked the lawyer.

Margaret glanced at the clock, the hands of which pointed to half-past twelve.

" Half an hour," she answered.

" Then, I will speak to you now. I shall not have time this afternoon."

He was standing with his back to the fire, and Margaret was in one of the large deep armchairs which graced either side of the fireplace.

" That will," he said, after a pause; " it

leaves you totally unprovided for. What
are you going to do?"

"I shall go to London. I have a friend
there."

"Yes, yes; but is he in a position to
help you? I mean, can he do more than
just point out a course to be taken, and
then leave you to go on alone?"

"Oh yes; he was my tutor. He will
help me, and show me what is best for me
to do."

He nodded his head.

"And until I hear from him," she went
on, "I should like to remain here, if I
may?" raising her eyes to his.

"Of course. All that is left in my
hands. I hope you will make this place
your home as long as will be convenient
to you. I do not suppose Mrs. Latimer
has any intention of leaving India. I dare

say she would be very glad if you would remain here altogether. If you like, I will write and lay the case before her."

"You are very kind, but please don't do anything of the kind. I should not like to live here in that way. It is nothing to me to leave this place. Indeed, if my grandfather had not died, I must have left this house when he recovered."

He nodded his head again; he was a man of few words. There was a long pause. Margaret began to think he did not mean to speak again, when he said suddenly—

"Your name was not mentioned in the will, Miss Terry. I do not know if you—— Can I be of any present use to you?"

Margaret flushed, for his kindness touched her.

"I cannot sufficiently thank you for your

kindness, Mr. Banks; but I have sufficient money for my present wants, and I hope to find work soon."

Here lunch was announced, and Mr. Banks, offering his arm to Margaret with old-fashioned chivalry, handed her into the dining-room.

Soon after lunch he went away, and Margaret was left alone in the silent house. She sat before the fire, thinking. She was going to write to Philip that evening, and she wanted to think before beginning her letter. For the first time since her grandfather's death she had leisure to think, and as she sat in the gathering dusk, for the afternoon had closed in early with a grey fog and driving, beating rain, she realized that that chapter of her life which dealt with Ash Fell would soon be closed.

She went over in her mind the time from

the moment when Dr. Hunter had said
"He is gone," to the present hour. Most
of all, she thought of the will, and then
her face flushed. It would be useless to
pretend that the will had not roused both
her anger and her disappointment. She
was angry because she knew the estate was
hers by right, and Margaret had a great
respect for right. She was disappointed
because all her dreams of benefiting the
tenants were at an end ; she could never
hope to carry out the smallest of her plans
for their good.

But she had left what was better than
anything she could have inherited from her
grandfather. He might take away wealth,
station, and power, but he could never
rob her of her independence. Though her
name had not been mentioned in the will,
though she might carry away nothing that

did not strictly belong to herself, she felt
very rich; and as she sat alone she pictured
her future life in London in glowing
colours.

The following morning Mrs. Entwistle
came in.   She seated herself opposite
Margaret, and began her business at once.

"Now, my dear, we must see what can
be done for you.   Of course you will have
to work now, and, after all, you have no
right to complain; you have had nineteen
years of holiday."

"I do not complain," said Margaret; "on
the contrary, I shall be very glad to work.
It is what I have always wished to do."

"That is very fortunate," replied her
visitor, blandly.   "And what do you think
of doing?   I suppose you will try to get
a situation as governess, or something of
that kind.   I have no doubt we shall meet

with something by-and-by. I must inquire
among my friends."

"Thank you," answered the girl; "but
I will not put you to so much trouble. I
am not going to be a governess. I am
going to London. I shall live there."

"Indeed!" said the other, stiffly. "How
do you propose to do that?"

"I have written to Mr. Welford; he will
tell me what to do."

"That was a very strange step to take
without consulting those who have your
welfare at heart. And you cannot go to
Mr. Welford."

"I shall go to his mother, I expect," said
the girl, not trying to hide her amusement.
"I have quite made up my mind,"
seeing that Mrs. Entwistle was going to
speak again.

"You are acting in a very bold, independent manner, which I cannot approve of at all," said the elder lady.

"I am independent; that is the great advantage."

Mrs. Entwistle did not stay much longer. Her parting words were—

"You know, Margaret, if you had played your cards well you might have been left with a handsome fortune."

To which Margaret made no reply.

The following morning Margaret heard from Philip. He was most anxious for her to come to London, and offered her a home with his mother as long as she chose to avail herself of it.

The letter put Margaret into the highest spirits. She decided to leave Ash Fell on the following day. The greater part of the time that remained to her she spent in packing up her things, and at night she

went to say good-bye to the place that had
been her home.

The stately rooms on the ground floor
raised no emotion in her, unless it was of
joy that she was leaving them for ever;
but when she had mounted the stairs and
reached the rooms where she and Philip
had lived, she felt her heart swell and her
eyes fill. She set down the lamp she
carried, and looked round the old sitting-
room. A thousand memories came over
her, blinding her eyes with tears. Though
twenty-four hours later she would again
have met her only friend, be speaking to
him or hearing his voice, she felt that the
old days were gone, that nothing could
bring them back.

"Nothing," she thought, "is ever the
same twice over." Though it was only a
year since Philip had himself said good-

bye to her in that same room, though they were going to meet again so soon, she dropped into a chair, leaned her head upon the old work-table, and cried bitterly.

The next morning she left Ash Fell, and from the railway carriage window waved a farewell to the village of which the last object she saw was "the little grey church on the windy hill," where her grandfather lay buried.

On the evening of that same day, three women were seated in the drawing-room of a house in one of the suburbs of London.

Mrs. Welford and her two daughters were awaiting the arrival of Margaret Terry. Mrs. Welford was but little altered since we saw her last, eleven years ago. Elsa and Madge were grown up, but, in spite of their taller stature, were little changed in character. Elsa was still gay and light of heart, as a butterfly sporting in the sun; Madge's face still wore its old troubled, careworn look.

The ladies were sitting in silence. Mrs. Welford and Madge were working; Elsa, who was the youngest and indulged, sat in the most comfortable chair in the room, deep in a three volume novel. Mrs. Welford herself broke the silence.

"What time did Philip say Miss Terry's train got in?"

"Quarter-past eight," said Madge, who always fulfilled the minor duties of life, such as answering superfluous questions, and the like.

Mrs. Welford looked at the clock, which struck half-past eight as she looked.

"We may expect them in a quarter of an hour, then, if the train is punctual," she said, speaking in slow, measured tones.

" What fun ! " cried Elsa, looking up from her book. "I am so glad she is coming. I am dying with curiosity to see her. I asked Philip the other day if she is pretty, and he smiled in that absent way he has, and said he had really never considered the point. She had always been Margaret to him. I long to see what she is like."

" There is a cab stopping at the door," said Madge, without raising her eyes from her work. Elsa was the only one of the party who showed any inclination to go out and meet the guest; neither did she get any further than the door, for her mother called her back, sharply bidding her not expose herself to the night air.

They heard Philip open the door with his latch-key, and his voice speaking to some one, who answered in sweet, full tones. Then he came in, and, turning round, they saw he was leading forward a tall girl, dressed in black, with a pale, beautiful face and golden hair, which her long journey had ruffled somewhat.

"Mother," said Philip, who looked very happy, "here is Margaret."

The girl advanced, and Mrs. Welford rose and, extending her hand, said—

"How do you do, Miss Terry? I hope you are not very cold after your long journey?"

Somewhat chilled by Mrs. Welford's frigid manner, Margaret turned involuntarily to the girls, to whom Philip introduced her. They acknowledged the introduction characteristically. Madge hurriedly shook hands, and, murmuring a few indistinct words, dropped her eyes again on to her work. Elsa kissed the new-comer's cheek, and poured forth a volley of welcoming words.

They were standing in front of the fire; one hand Margaret held to the blaze, the other Philip was holding in his and gently chafing it.

" Miss Terry must be starving," said Elsa. " Supper is just ready. Miss Terry, will you go to your room now, or wait until afterwards.

" I will go now," taking her gloves from the mantelpiece where she had laid them.

" I will show you the way," said Elsa; and the two girls left the room together.

A few minutes later they were seated at supper, and a brisk conversation was going on. Philip and Margaret had so much to talk about, and Elsa joined in so persistently, that the silence of the other two was not noticed.

Margaret went to bed early, and Philip left for his rooms a few minutes later, saying he would call in the course of the following morning.

" Well! " said Elsa, when the party was reduced to its primitive number of three, " what do you think of her ? I think she is most beautiful. I could look at her for hours."

" She is good-looking," said Mrs. Welford, dispassionately ; " but her manner is more free and independent than I care to see in so young a girl."

" What do you think, Madge ? " turning to her sister.

" I ? Oh, I don't know. I hardly looked at her. I like her ; I can understand what Philip meant by saying she had always been Margaret. She looks as though, however other people might change, she would always be herself."

Elsa laughed. "You see," she said. "she wears no crape. That is one of Philip's ideas. You know, he would do away with mourning if he could. I expect we shall find he has filled her head with all his wild ideas."

CHAPTER X.

"Get leave to work
In this world : 'tis the best you get at all."

THE following morning, as Margaret sat
with the girls and Mrs. Welford after
breakfast, some one was heard running up
the door-steps.

"That is Mr. Welford," said Margaret,
quickly ; and Elsa looked up and laughed.

"Do you know his step ?" she asked ;
"none of us do."

Philip entered the room. He greeted his
mother and sisters with a kiss, and shook
hands with Margaret, telling her she looked

a hundred times better than the night before.

"I hardly knew you as you stood on the platform," he concluded.

"I knew you directly. I had thought of very little but meeting you all through the journey."

"There is a compliment, Phil," said Elsa, in delight.

"Margaret and I are above compliments," said Philip, smiling as he drew his chair close up to that on which the girl was sitting. "How did you leave every one at Ash Fell—Mrs. Entwistle, for instance?"

"Mrs. Entwistle!" cried Margaret, laughing. "She left me, and in a very angry frame of mind. She had come with the intention of offering me a refuge in her house, until together we had found me a

situation as governess. Was she not
kind ? "

Philip laughed.

"Just like Mrs. Entwistle," he said.
" What did you say to her ? "

She told him. When she had finished,
he said—

" Now, put on your things, and come out
with me, if you are rested, and we will
talk business."

She did his bidding, and they went out
together. He took her to the National
Gallery, which they had almost to themselves, and there they began to talk.

" Tell me first, Margaret," he said,
" whether you have any money."

"I have a great deal," she answered.
" Forty pounds."

" That is not much," he said, smiling.

" But enough to go on with. I shall

get work soon, and shall be able to keep myself. How delightful that will be!"

"You cannot guess, I am sure, how I got my money," she said, after a pause.

"Did you sell your old dresses?" he asked. "I have heard of girls raising funds in that way."

"I should certainly not have got forty pounds for mine. I sold 'Miss Terry's jewelry,'" she said, laughing. "I felt such a weight off my mind when I had got rid of it."

"I hope 'Miss Terry's jewelry' did not include your watch and chain?" he said, smiling.

"Of course not; nor your diamond ring either," she said, alluding to presents from Philip on successive birthdays.

Then they began to talk seriously. It was settled that Margaret should have lodgings and take pupils, until her name was sufficiently well known for her to be able to stand alone. After that, Philip took her to his old friend, the dealer. He had found a ready market for the things Philip had sent him a year before, and Margaret undertook to keep him constantly supplied.

"How fortunate I am!" she said, as they turned their steps homewards; "and it is all owing to you. If I had been alone, I should have had such difficulties to encounter; now they are all smoothed away."

"There is no difficulty in helping people who are willing to be helped," said Philip, sagely.

They reached home just in time for dinner, and as Margaret seated herself at table, Philip, looking at her, was struck anew by her great beauty. She was roused and excited with the consciousness that she was free, that she was going to begin a new life, and that the future lay bright and hopeful before her. She was feeling, as well, the elation that always attends one's first visit to a large town ; the incessant life in the streets, the gay shops, the lighted lamps, all impressed her, and made her feel as though she had been taken into a new world.

Philip did not intend Margaret to leave his mother's house until she had a prospect of being able to support herself in lodgings. A month passed before the girl left Clapham, and during that month she saw and learned a great deal. Philip came every day, spending his time with his family, or taking Margaret, and sometimes his sisters, out. They went to Kensington, to the British Museum, to the National Gallery, and to concerts innumerable. On such occasions they were generally alone, Elsa seldom accompanying them on what she called their "intellectual expeditions."

Margaret got on pretty well with her hostess and her daughters. She felt sorry for Madge, and Elsa amused her. She had seen and known very few girls in her quiet life, and she was sometimes rather surprised to find the difference which existed between herself and the girls she now met. Elsa and Madge, on their side, considered Margaret rather in the light of a curiosity, and were never tired of asking questions concerning the life Margaret and Philip had led together.

"Tell me," Elsa said one day, "what you used to do when Philip was your tutor. Were you happy?"

"Oh yes," said Margaret, readily. "He

was so kind, it would have been impossible not to be happy."

" I suppose you did a great many lessons, you seem to know everything."

" We did not do lessons like they do in schools. When I learned botany, we used to go for a picnic among the hills, and botanize there. Most of the things I know were learned when we were either riding or walking; we had no regular lesson hours, or books, or routine, or anything; we did just what we liked at the moment. I shall never forget a lesson in geology that Mr. Welford gave me one afternoon when we were sitting on the moors."

Margaret sat looking dreamily into the fire. Those happy bygone days seemed to come back to her as vividly as if she had been living in them.

When Margaret had been at Clapham a

month, she induced Philip to let her go
into lodgings. She was not very happy
in her present home. The girl was no
favourite with Mrs. Welford, and she knew
it. The elder lady did not like what she
called Margaret's "freedom and independence," and she showed her dislike by an
unbending rigidity of demeanour. Mrs.
Welford forgot how different was the life
Margaret had led from that led by most
girls, and she was constantly advising,
reprimanding, and directing in a way that
chafed the girl's quick, impulsive temper,
and made her vexed and impatient, though
she tried not to show her feelings. She
was fond of the girls, and gave them a
general invitation to visit her whenever
they choose.

Margaret's friendship for Philip only
grew warmer : she was very grateful to

him for his kindness during the time she had been his mother's guest. He had soon seen how matters stood, and all his efforts had been directed to softening his mother's prejudices, and helping Margaret to make light of them.

Before Margaret left Clapham she had advanced so far as to call her tutor by his Christian name. Elsa had brought the change about, and was delighted with the result of her labours; and though Margaret had been a little shy at first, when the change was effected it seemed in some way to draw Philip nearer to her.

CHAPTER XI.

" Ah! let us make no claim
  On life's incognizable sea,
  To too exact a steering of our way;
  Let us not fret, and fear to miss our aim,
  If some fair coast has lured us to make stay,
  Or some friend hailed us to keep company."

FOR some time after Margaret began her new life, no change occurred to disturb the even tenor of her way. Her pupils came, and she gave them their lessons; she worked diligently in the workroom that opened out of her pretty sitting-room. Some of her lessons she gave at the homes of her pupils, and in this way made some new acquaintances, though Philip remained her only friend. Hers was not a nature that made friends quickly. She was long in holding out the right hand of fellowship, but her hand, once held out, was never withdrawn.

She had been living alone for five months. It was now May, and every-where out of London the country was looking almost at its best; even in the metropolis there was a sneaking feeling of springtide in the atmosphere.

This May afternoon was exceptionally fine, and the sun shone brightly in at one of Margaret's windows, which was wide open to admit as much of the sweet spring air as possible. She herself was standing by the table, working busily. The floor was covered with little chips and shavings, and the room was strewn with tools of all sorts and sizes suitable for her work. She was standing with her back to the light, and the sun just caught the gleam of her golden hair as she bent over her tools. She had left off her black dresses, and the one which now clothed her tall figure was of a soft gray colour, which suited her well.

As she worked, a quick step ran up the stairs, and some one gave a sharp rap on the door.

" Philip's knock," she thought; and she said quickly—

" Come in."

Her face wore a smile as the young man entered, and she held out her hand.

" How do you do, Philip ? It is a long time since you have been here."

" I have been intending to come for days," he answered, throwing himself into the broad window-seat, " but I have always been prevented from coming all the way."

" You are here now, so the rest does not matter," she said, contentedly, leaving her work for a moment.

" Do you know," said Philip, after a little pause, " it struck me as I came in just now that you looked rather desolate. I hope the girls do not neglect you."

" On the contrary, they come very often —quite as often as Mrs. Welford will let them, I am` sure. It is the kinder of them, as sometimes when they get here I am too busy to talk to them."

" How do you think Madge is looking ? " asked Philip, suddenly.

" I do not think she looks happy," she said, slowly though decidedly.

" No," said her brother; " she is too much under my mother's rule to be that.

No one can associate happiness with my mother."

Margaret was silent, and presently Philip said—

"I came to ask you to go out with me. Are you too busy?"

"Much," she answered, regretfully. "How I should have liked to go! but I must send this home to-night. It is for a birthday present to-morrow."

"What is it?"

"This is a glove-box; the handkerchief-case is on that table."

"It is very beautiful," said Philip, taking it up and examining it. "I think you have improved."

"I know I have; I am very much pleased with this."

"And you can't leave it to come out with me?"

" Impossible.   I   have   some   news   for
you."

" What may it be ? "

" You   remember   Mr.   Bannister,   who
lives   some   miles   from   Ash   Fell ?   Mr.
Terry   knew   him;   he   came   to   a   dinner-
party once.   He and his wife are building
a church;   they are spending a great deal
of   money   upon   it.   It   is   one   of   those
ritualistic   places,   the   pulpit,   the   stalls,   and
chancel   screen,   are   to   be   in   carved oak,   and
they want——"

" You   to   do   it," interrupted   Philip,
impulsively.   " My dear girl, how delightful for you ! "

" Is   it   not   charming ?   They   want   me
to go at once, but will wait my convenience.
Such   a   nice   letter   from   Mrs.   Bannister !
Read   it; "   and   she   handed   him   an   open
sheet   of   paper.   " You   see,"   she   went   on,

"they want me to stay in the house all the time. I remember Mrs. Entwistle said they had a delightful house, and generally lots of people staying there."

"I am very glad," said Philip, warmly. "When shall you go?"

"I cannot go until next month. I have work which will keep me here until then; but in June I shall go. I am very glad I shall spend the summer in the country, after all."

"I suppose you have no idea how long you will be away?"

"No, of course. I cannot even guess until I have seen the church."

She was working again as she spoke, her deft fingers handling her tools with perfect ease and skill.

Philip sat and watched her for some little time, then he said—

" I have nothing particular to do this evening. If you will let me, I will stay here, and we will try to bring one of our old evenings back again."

She assented eagerly, and they sat talking until Margaret had finished her work, packed it up, and sent it off; then Philip made her get one of their favourite books, and they read together until the light failed them.

Philip stayed till late, and when he was gone, Margaret sat by the low table which held her reading lamp, and began to think of the work in store for her.

She was very ambitious, and very desirous that her work should always aim at a high ideal. A great deal of the carving she saw in shops, and in the few houses where she visited, often made her feel how easy it was for untrained, unskilled workers to debase an art. With the enthusiasm natural to her youth and temperament, she had been determined that her work should be such as to raise the character and tone of her art; she would do nothing that . was not perfect in its way.

A month later, she said "Good-bye" to Philip and went north to Fencehurst, the united village of which Mr. and Mrs. Bannister were the presiding geniuses.

It was a long journey, but, during the latter part at least, a very beautiful one. As the train rushed swiftly through the hilly, picturesque country, Margaret's heart began to beat fast with the pleasure and excitement of visiting her native Yorkshire. The hills were not yet clad in purple, but they were green with bracken and yellow with gorse. The rushing, tumbling streams, which threw themselves headlong down the narrow gorges studded with hardy birch and mountain ash, were fresh and sparkling as when Margaret had wandered by them the summer before.

A phaeton had been sent to the station to meet her, and the two miles to Fence-hurst were soon covered. Margaret was met in the hall by Mrs. Bannister, who gave her a warm welcome, and accompanied her to her room, saying that dinner would be ready in half an hour.

When Margaret, a few minutes before seven o'clock, entered the drawing-room, she found it full of people. A large party was staying at Fencehurst, for Mr. and Mrs. Bannister, in spite of their ritualistic pro-clivities, were fond of the good things of this life, and seldom spent much time alone.

Margaret, as she had told Philip, had seen Mr. Bannister at Ash Fell, where he had sat at her grandfather's table, and paid a great deal of attention to his young hostess. She found also Mr. Barton at Fencehurst; indeed, he took her in to dinner, and did not let pass the opportunity of asking after the Rev. Adolphe.

In the drawing-room, Mrs. Bannister seated herself by Margaret, and talked to her about the new church. She was very enthusiastic, and said she had numbers of plans, which she would submit to Miss Terry in the morning.

" Of course," she said, " you will not be able to tell all at once how long it will take you to do the carving, but Mr. Bannister and I hope you will make Fencehurst your home, so long as you are here."

"You are very kind,'" said Margaret; and Mrs. Bannister went away, wondering what had induced Mr. Terry to treat his grand-daughter as he had done.

The following day Mr. Bannister took Margaret to the church. It lay about a quarter of a mile from the lodge gates, and was a beautiful building of pure white stone, with a tall, tapering spire. Mr. Bannister unlocked the door, and they went in. Inside, the church was exquisite. All the windows were of the finest painted glass; the chancel steps and floor were of pure white marble, while the altar literally blazed with colour; the woodwork was all of shining black oak. Mr. Bannister called largely upon her for admiration, but to Margaret's unaccustomed eyes it looked more like a fairy palace than a church, and she frankly said so.

Then they began to talk about the carving, and after Mr. Bannister had listened to Margaret for some time he said—

"You have a genius for these things, Miss Terry. Our church will be known far and wide, and your work will go down to posterity."

She flushed, half with pleasure at the thought which flattered her ambition, half with another feeling which she could hardly analyze.

"I will begin my preparations this afternoon," she said, as they turned to leave the building.

"I don't think you will be allowed to do that," he answered, laughing. "I believe my wife has organized a drive or something for this afternoon, and I know she intends you to make one of the party."

So in the afternoon, instead of beginning her work, Margaret cast in her lot with the rest of the visitors at Fencehurst, and spent the golden summer afternoon among the hills.

Margaret soon found that, even allowing for several hours' hard work every day, it would take her three months to do what she had to do at the church. She told Mrs. Bannister, adding—

"And, as I cannot think of trespassing upon your hospitality for so long, I must look about for lodgings."

But Mrs. Bannister and her husband, whom she called in to her support, were resolute in opposing any such arrangement. They were determined she should stay with them until her work was done.

So Margaret stayed, nothing loth, and felt happier day by day.

CHAPTER XII.

" Taller he showed than any by a head,
   Great-limbed, broad-shouldered, mightier far than
      all,
   But soft of speech."

MARGARET had been at Fencehurst a fortnight. Some of the people who had been
there at her arrival still lingered at that
pleasant house; others had gone, and fresh
faces came in their place. They were all
pleasant people who stayed at Fencehurst:
it was noted for the delightful parties that
gathered within its ivied walls.

It was a sultry evening in July, and
Margaret sat in her rooms, resting from her

work for a few minutes before beginning
to dress for dinner, and she was arranging
the flowers, heavy tea-roses, which she was
going to wear that evening.

Mr. Barton, who had taken her in to
dinner with unfailing regularity for the
last fortnight, had left that morning, and
she was idly wondering who would be her
cavalier that evening. She had heard that
some one else was expected that afternoon;
had even heard his name, but had forgotten
what it was. Perhaps he would take
her in.

When she went downstairs she found
the drawing-room almost empty; few
women took so short a time to "adorn"
themselves as Margaret, and the majority
were still upstairs. She went forward to
one of the windows, an immense bay, in
which a semicircular seat was placed, and,

sitting down, leaned back and turned over
the leaves of a book some one had left on
the seat. Among the men scattered about
the room a distinct though subdued murmur
of conversation was going on, and Margaret
caught some of the words.

" Has Saxenholme come yet ? Has any
one seen Saxenholme ? " were the inquiries
being buzzed about the room, and as she
heard them she remembered that Saxenholme was the name of the man who was
to arrive that afternoon.

Insensibly the room filled. It was nearly
half-past seven, and some people out of the
neighbourhood were dining with them that
night. Margaret from her corner watched
the guests come in and settle down into
little groups for conversation.

Before the fireplace several men were
standing, talking to a tall man, who, as

his face was strange to her, Margaret concluded was the new guest. He was a man
immensely tall and proportionately broad.
His hair was only a shade darker than her
own. So far as she could see, his eyes
were black, and his complexion was singularly tanned, as though he had been much
exposed to suns hotter than we are accustomed to in England. His eyes were
singularly quick and piercing ; indeed, his
face had such an attraction for Miss Terry
that she found it difficult to withdraw her
eyes from it. At the same time, she had
an odd feeling that though the man seemed
completely engrossed in his conversation
with his companions, yet he was all the
time watching her as she was watching
him.

" He seems a great favourite," she
thought ; "and in spite of his keen eyes

and quick voice, he looks kind, and as though he would never do an unmanly deed."

Presently she saw Mrs. Bannister go up to the group on the hearth, exchange a few words with one of the men, speak to the stranger, and finally lead him away captive in the direction of the window where she was sitting.

The lady seemed to be talking earnestly; the stranger was listening with an amused, half-bantering expression on his face. When they reached Margaret's side, Mrs. Bannister said—

"Miss Terry, I want to introduce my friend, Mr. Oswald Saxenholme. Mr. Saxenholme, Miss Terry."

Saxenholme bowed; but Margaret, impelled by some instinct for which she could not quite account, held out her hand, which Oswald took in his and held for half a second.

Mrs. Bannister lingered near them for a moment, and then moved away. Oswald dropped into the seat by Margaret's side, saying—

"What a delightful woman Mrs. Bannister is!"

"Is she not?" cried Margaret, turning quickly to him, to find his eyes fixed upon her. "I never met a woman I liked half so well."

"Have you known her long?"

"Only during the last fortnight, but that is quite long enough to find out how good she is."

"Yes," he answered; "she is very good. I have known her ever since we were both children, and we have always been friends. I do not recollect a single quarrel."

At that moment dinner was announced.

"I am to have the pleasure of taking you down to dinner," he said, rising and offering his arm to Margaret; and she looked up with a start, for she had forgotten where she was.

"Are you staying here long?" asked Oswald, when dinner was half over.

"Until I have done my work," she answered.

"Your work?" he repeated; and then went on hastily, "But, pardon me, I have no business to ask you anything like that. That was a most impertinent question."

"Not at all. I am working for Mr. and Mrs. Bannister. I am carving the wood-work in the church."

"Indeed? Are you, too, helping to build up the Church of the future?"

"Is that the Church of the future?" she

asked; and Oswald's answer led them into a long discussion, whither we will not follow them.

When they were sitting in the drawing-room after dinner, Margaret crossed over to Mrs. Bannister, who was alone, and asked—

" Who is that Mr. Saxenholme who took me in to dinner ? "

" Who is Oswald ? " said Mrs. Bannister. " He is Oswald. To people who know him that expresses everything."

" Doubtless. But I don't know him, so that to say 'he is Oswald' means nothing to me."

" Where shall I begin ? " said her hostess. " Did you ever hear of 'Saxenholme Brothers' ? "

Margaret shook her head.

" They were bankers—they have been bankers ever since banks began to exist.

The bank and the name have come down to posterity, though the Brothers have not. At present it is 'Saxenholme and Sons,' and they have the largest private bank in London."

"And is this Mr. Oswald Saxenholme one of the sons?"

"Yes; the youngest. There are two of them. Mr. Saxenholme and his eldest son are in the business. Oswald, lazy fellow, does nothing."

"How intolerable!" exclaimed Margaret.

Mrs. Bannister laughed.

"Every one has not your horror of idleness. But I am wronging Oswald in your eyes. When I say he does nothing, I mean nothing in the business. They are immensely wealthy people. Oswald has all his mother's money, and he spends all his time on his pet hobby."

"I am glad he has some occupation, if it is only a hobby. What does he do?"

"How sarcastically you speak! Oswald is a geographer. I have known him since he was a child, and his one passion is geography. Even when I first knew him his greatest happiness lay in reading travels and geography. Later on, he thirsted to be an explorer, or to join a party of explorers. I believe he either has offered, or is going to offer, himself as commander of that party that is leaving England at the end of the summer, for the exploration of the interior of Africa."

"What modesty! Will nothing less than the command suit him?"

"Oh, he is very ambitious; as ambitious as you are."

Margaret coloured a little, but she laughed

too, and Mrs. Bannister left her to speak to some one else.

Margaret sat thinking. Suddenly a voice at her side said—

" Mrs. Bannister has been telling me about your carving in the church. May I not see it?"

The plain, straightforward question struck Margaret favourably, after all the compliments and amateur criticism she had been hearing of late, and she answered readily—

" I shall be very glad to show you all I have done, whenever you like to-morrow."

" To-morrow!" with an accent of disappointment. " I really doubt whether I can wait till to-morrow; it would be throwing away a night's rest. I had hoped you would show it me to-night."

" To-night!" she said, in some surprise.

"I do not think we could see it; it will be dark in the church now."

"Do come," he said, persuasively. And then, changing his tone, he went on quickly, "Come, Miss Terry; I see a lady approaching whom I know of old. She is going to force us to join a fearful and wonderful round game, which no one knows but herself, and which it is impossible to learn; I believe she invented it herself. Come!"

He started up as he spoke, and went hastily in the direction of an open French window. Almost without knowing what she did, Margaret followed him, and a moment later they stood together on the terrace.

"That was well done," said Oswald, laughing. "I often wonder why Miss Langton comes here. She is the only disagreeable person one ever meets at Fence-hurst."

When they entered the church, Margaret pointed out her work, and Oswald peered round in the dusk, and was forced at last to say, with a laugh—

"You were quite right, Miss Terry; I cannot see it at all. I must come again in daylight."

They did not stay long in the church, but once out of doors again they lingered. It was such a perfect June night, so warm and so still, and the flowers sent out such a soft, haunting perfume, it seemed a shame to go indoors, even to sit in a drawing-room lighted with the softest of candles and lamps. Oswald and Margaret paced the terrace almost in silence, though there was no question raised of going indoors, or of joining any of the laughing, chattering

groups scattered about the garden. Gradually the people went indoors, and Margaret
and Oswald had been for some time alone
when the former suddenly said—

"I had no idea every one had gone in.
It must be getting quite late. Let us go
in, too; the air is getting chill."

And with that they passed through the
still open window and returned to the
drawing-room.

It was late when they separated for the
night, and yet Margaret felt no inclination
to sleep. The candles on her dressing-
table burned with a soft shimmering light,
and the blind was down. She drew it
up, and, throwing the window wide open,
leaned far out into the still night. Her
heart was beating fast, and her pulses
throbbed. Her whole being was roused
and excited; she had never in her life felt

as she did this night. Her thoughts
naturally turned to Oswald Saxenholme.
He had spent nearly the whole evening at
her side, and the echo of his last words
seemed still sounding in her ears. She
thought he was the handsomest man she
had ever seen. Among all the men who
had frequented her grandfather's house, she
remembered none with so goodly a presence
as his; none who bore his head so proudly
aloft, or who looked so far removed from
all meanness or littleness of soul. She had
never heard a voice that rang so true and
brave in her ears; never seen eyes that
looked into hers with such an open, fearless gaze.

So she sat by the window dreaming, and
the short June night was almost over when
she shut the window and turned to undress.

CHAPTER XIII.

> " So she moved
> Amid them all, a thing beloved
> Of earth and heaven ; could she be
> Made for his sole felicity ? "

THE following morning, as Margaret was at work in the church, she heard the door open and some one come up the aisle. Looking up, she saw that it was Mr. Saxenholme.

" Good morning ! " he said, holding out his hand. " It is half-past eleven, and the first time we have met to-day."

" You were not down when I had breakfast," she said, when she had returned his greeting.

"You must have been very early. I kept expecting you to come into the dining-room, but you never came. At last I thought it possible you might be here, so I came to see."

"I generally breakfast alone," she said.

"That must be very lonely," he said, with perfect gravity.

They talked for a long time. Margaret told her visitor of the amusing criticism sometimes passed upon her work by the guests at Fencehurst. From that they passed to other subjects, and almost before Margaret knew what she was saying, she had put Oswald into possession of the chief details of her past and present life. When she had finished speaking, she was seized with astonishment that she could have talked so openly to such a complete stranger as was Oswald Saxenholme.

When Oswald spoke again, it was on quite a different subject, and he presently abandoned his lazy attitude, and began to wander up and down the church, apparently examining it.

After this, they spent a great deal of time together. They talked, argued, and disputed, and were sometimes on the verge of quarrelling. Margaret had by this time learned a great deal of Oswald's history and occupations. From answers given to her own questions, and also from information volunteered by himself, she learned that here he had no abiding city, that he spent most of his time in travelling, and that he made his father's house in London his head-quarters. He told her, too, a great deal about the expedition just being organized for the exploration of the interior of Africa. He said he had almost made up his mind to join it.

"I am not bound so that I could not draw back if anything happened to prevent my going," he said one day; "but I expect I shall go. I have nothing to keep me in England, and it would be a splendid opportunity for distinguishing one's self."

"When do they leave England?" she asked.

"In the autumn sometime. I am not quite sure when."

"How long are they going to be absent?"

"Of course, they cannot tell; but I believe they have fixed three years as the furthest limit of time."

She did not speak, but went on working

with a steady hand, though her heart was heavy with the thought, "He is eager to go. There is nothing to keep him in England. He would be away three years, which I suppose I should spend in growing older and duller and more stupid. Why did he ever come near me?"

Looking up, she said, speaking coldly from the very intensity of her feeling—

"You are standing in my light, Mr. Saxenholme. Do you mind standing on one side?"

He gave her a quick look as he did her bidding, and she went on—

"I suppose even the most inveterately idle people must have something to occupy themselves with."

"Do you consider me inveterately idle, Miss Terry?"

"You have always described yourself as

being without any employment, and I never see you do anything here."

" You do not like lazy people, I think ? "

" I despise them," she said, quickly, her mouth growing scornful.

His handsome face flushed a little, though he laughed as he said—

" I believe you are right. Mrs. Bannister is always imploring me to work in some way. She threatens me with the most terrible penalties if I do not reform. What do you think she told me the other day ? "

" I cannot imagine."

" And your voice say you do not care to know, that I have bored you long enough; but I am rude and selfish, and I shall go on boring you. I want to know if you agree with her, because I value your judgment very highly."

" You are very kind."

He laughed unrestrainedly, and there was a pause, which he broke by asking—

"You do not ask what Mrs. Bannister said."

"I do not care to hear."

"But I am going to tell you. She said ' that though I thought myself very fascinating '—you see, I do not hesitate to repeat her most malicious slanders—' I should find no woman worthy of the name who would consent to be the wife of such a lazy, shiftless fellow as I am.'"

He was looking straight at Margaret, as she stood with her eyes fixed on her work. She did not speak, and he waited until a light of amusement came into his eyes; but he was quite grave as he asked—

"You do not say if you think she was right."

"I have no opinion on the matter."

Still she did not meet his eyes. He shifted his position, and went on—

" This is most lamentable ! I assure you, Mrs. Bannister's words cut me up a great deal, and I wanted to hear if you agreed with her. I might doubt her justice, but not hers and yours. I *should* like to know what you think ? "

" It would take too long to tell."

" I hardly know what to make of that answer ; let me ask you something else. I begin to wonder if it is too late for me to reform. I am seven and twenty ; tell me whether you think there is any chance for me, if I begin at once."

Her heart was beating so that she could hardly speak. She could not tell what he meant, whether he was in earnest or only amusing himself at her expense ; but she could not resist the influence of his gaze and his persuasive voice, and she answered slowly—

"That is for yourself to decide, I think."

The words had hardly left her mouth, and he was going to reply, when the church door opened, and two or three of the Fencehurst party entered, talking.

Margaret hailed their appearance with mingled emotions of relief and disappointment, which showed themselves in the flush that spread over her fair face. Oswald looked bored, but he raised himself into an upright position, and greeted the newcomers with his wonted cheerfulness.

A few days after this, Oswald announced his intention of going to London for a few days. He felt restless and dissatisfied. He could not tell whether Margaret cared for him or not, and he could not make up his mind to ask her.

He did not know whether to come back to Fencehurst or not. Was it worth his while coming back? He could not tell. At last he hit upon an expedient for finding out. When Margaret and he stood alone in the garden, he said suddenly—

"I am going away to-morrow, Miss Terry."

His eyes were fixed upon her face as he spoke. He was watching for the slightest change in expression or manner, and only a man watching as he did could have detected the very slight increase of colour in her face, and the almost imperceptible tremor in her voice, as she answered—

"So soon, Mr. Saxenholme? Is it not rather sudden?"

She did not look at him as she spoke, and Oswald thought in triumph that it must be because she was afraid of betraying more than she wished to show.

"It is rather sudden. The fact is, I ought to have gone long ago, but I could not tear myself away; and now I avail myself of a very peremptory business call to do what is only my duty, though I am unreasonable enough to regard it as a hardship."

He smiled as he spoke. She smiled too, though she said—

"Are you coming back? Shall we not see you again?"

He paused before he answered. Should he say, "I will come back on one condition—that you promise to be my wife;" but instead, he said—

"I may come back; I am not sure."

The next day he went; but at the end of a fortnight he returned, and until he

came back, Margaret did not know how completely she had missed him. He seemed to
have grown into and become a part of her
life, and the consciousness that it was so
disturbed her and caused her some anxiety.

"I am very foolish," she thought, "to
attach myself to what I cannot keep, and
to throw myself so much into the lives of
people I shall probably never see again. I
will not do it. I will try to forget
Oswald Saxenholme and the three months
I have spent here, though they have been
very happy ones."

But the process of forgetting advanced
but slowly, as Oswald was always with her,
always talking to her; and meanwhile
the days and weeks passed away, and her
work grew ever nearer completion.

END OF VOL. I.

www.ingramcontent.com/pod-product-compliance
Lightning Source LLC
Chambersburg PA
CBHW030814020726
47499CB00006B/1912